Brushes with Greatness

D1534828

: 05583

920
.009
04
Bru

Brushes with greatness : an antology of chance
encounters with celebrities / edited by Russell
Banks, Michael Ondaatje and David Young. --
Toronto : Coach House Press, c1989.
145 p. : port. -- (Big bang books)

03638022   ISBN:0889103496 (pbk.)

1. Celebrities - Anecdotes. 2. Fame - Anecdotes. I.
Banks, Russell, 1940- II. Ondaatje, Michael, 1943-
III. Young, David, 1946-

224   89OCT02   06/he   1-00933554

Brushes with Greatness

An anthology of chance encounters
with celebrities

edited by
Russell Banks, Michael Ondaatje
and David Young

BIG BANG

B O O K S

COACH HOUSE PRESS

TORONTO

© Copyright Coach House Press 1989

Published with the assistance of the Canada Council,
the Ontario Arts Council, and the Ontario Ministry
of Culture and Communications.

All authors' royalties from the sale of this Big Bank Book
are being donated to Amnesty International.

A special thanks to Monica Penner.

Cover design: Gordon Robertson.
Printed in Canada at Coach House Press, Toronto.
Tom Jones photo: C.W. Skarstedt Sr.

Canadian Cataloguing in Publication Data

Brushes with greatness

(A big bang book)
ISBN 0-88910-349-6

1. Celebrities – Anecdotes. 2. Fame – Anecdotes.
I. Banks, Russell, 1940– . II. Ondaatje, Michael, 1943– .
III. Young, David, 1946– .

CT105.B78 1989 920'.009'04 C89-094947-6

Of the Great and Famous Ever-to-be-honored Knight,
Sir Francis Drake, and of My Little-Little Self

The Dragon that our seas did raise his crest
And brought back heaps of gold unto his nest,
Unto his foes more terrible than thunder,
Glory of his age, after-ages' wonder,
Excelling all those that excelled before –
It's feared we shall have none such any more –
Effecting all, he sole did undertake,
Valiant, just, wise, mild, honest, godly Drake.
This man when I was little I did meet
As he was walking up Totnes' long street.
He asked me whose I was. I answered him.
He asked me if his good friend were within.
A fair red orange in his hand he had;
He gave it me, whereof I was right glad,
Takes and kissed me, and prays, 'God bless my boy,'
Which I record with comfort to this day.
Could he on me have breathéd with his breath
His gifts, Elias-like, after his death,
Then had I been enabled for to do
Many brave things I have a heart unto.
I have as great desire as e'er had he
To joy, annoy, friends, foes; but 'twill not be.

    – Robert Hayman

Did she put on his knowledge with his power
Before the indifferent beak could let her drop?

    – W.B. Yeats, *Leda and the Swan*

Contents

Introduction

Russell Banks

There are as many ways of looking at these stories (and what else should we call them, but stories?) as there are of looking at a black-bird, but a few general observations may be useful here. For who among us has not at least once told of a brush with greatness, whether his own or some lucky friend's, and having told it once, told it again and again, embellishing, editing, shaping and sharpening the story, until the desired effect was obtained? And what *was* that desired effect – beyond cutting through another boring dinner party conversation ('I say, that broccoli reminds me of the time I saw Princess Di naked ...')? Awe? Admiration? Fear and pity? Consolation? Laughter? Any and, at times, all of the above, I think – just as with stories, the 'fictional' kind.

So, to begin with: Reader Beware. Read these first-person accounts of encounters of the third kind as you would a short story by Raymond Carver or Jorge Luis Borges; i.e., keep always in mind the possibility that the narrator is unreliable and that the point of the story is something other than what the narrator says or seems to hope it is. For we have not checked the historical accuracy of these stories. Some of our contributors offered evidence, autographs of the brushee, photographs of the brusher and brushee taken by a nervous friend – talismans and relics, like portions of the True Cross – the sort of thing, unfortunately, that can be forged. How do we know that Joyce Carol Oates did not herself produce Mohammed Ali's bold signature? Thus we have been unable (as well as unwilling) to verify if, for instance, Sonja Skarstedt did in fact meet the soul-crooner Tom Jones, if Lionel Kearns met Fidel Castro or William Murphy met The Dalai Lama. As it happens, we received no accounts of someone's having brushed Jesus Christ, Shakespeare or Napoleon, which would have given us ... pause. But we might as well have included it anyhow, so long as the writer managed to make his or her account of the brush amusing, interesting or moving, or if we thought it added somehow to the overall mix. Actually, we were somewhat disappointed that there were no brushes with Jesus, Shakespeare or Napoleon. But then, this is a material age, in which the gods are demotic, just folks like you and me, only more so: thus the immanence of Fame, perhaps, the social use of Celebrity and its transience – for we do, after all, still seem to need gods. We just want them mortal, like us, which makes the pool of candidates long and wide, if a bit shallow.

The idea for this book originated among friends late one night in Toronto, over table and a few bottles of cabernet, as I recall, when one of us, à propos of nothing in particular, or so it seemed, told a story that we later came to recognize as a major type in the genre, The Sex God(dess) Validates the Brusher's Sexual Prowess. In this type, commonly told by middle-aged males, the brusher is usually portrayed as an adolescent – unworldly, insecure, unappreciated – regardless of his age at the time of the encounter, and the brushee, whose public identity is associated with Eros, recognizes the sexual reality of the narrator merely by means of a glance or an enigmatic word or two. (See William Matthews' meeting with Anita O'Day for a sophisticated variant, in which the brushee's public identity as a jazz singer, a 'thrush,' helps characterize the brusher as hip, smokey, laid-back, the envy of every intellectually precocious adolescent male who ever got turned down by a cheerleader.) It is common for this exchange to take place unobserved or in private, which makes it easy to lie about and thus popular among men sitting around over wine late at night. It may have been Young's apocryphal meeting with Marie MacDonald, or my version, told as if it happened to myself, of novelist Nicholas Delbanco's meeting with Marilyn Monroe (printed here and this time attributed accurately, and with my apologies, to Delbanco), or Ondaatje's dim memory of having established eye-contact in Manhattan with Marlene Dietrich. Whichever story came first, the others quickly followed – these were men talking, after all, and given the form of story being employed that night, they may have felt compelled to compete. We all know how that goes. (As Eddie Murphy says, 'It's a dick thing, don't try to understand it.')

There were others at the table that night, and soon everyone was telling of his or her chance encounter with someone famous, telling it with irony, humour, awe or sadness, depending on the identity of the person brushed and the narrator's particular emotional needs at the moment of telling. It was a social occasion; at that time we recognized no genre or sub-genres. The semiotics came later. We were merely a group of old friends, men and women, telling stories, a lot like the ones in this anthology. What immediately became clear, however, was that *everyone* had such a story and told it with intensity. It carried significance for the teller, and the way in which it got told, for better or worse, created in the listener, who was required only to know who the brushee was, an emotionally charged response (not always the one desired, however). Although the stories varied in length, the encounters themselves were brief. Friendships with the famous, continuing relationships of any kind, did not interest us. We did not discriminate between pop singers and moralists, athletes and artists, legendary chefs and venal politicians – such differences merely provided venues for irony or grief, humour or wonder, envy or instruction: they were, in a sense, formal parameters that organized the telling. The template was simple: Once upon a time, I, who am not famous, met someone who is famous, and there was an obscure but personally significant meaning in the encounter, and its nature will become obvious when you know whom I met and how. It did not matter that several of the people at the table that night might themselves be considered famous (if not at the level of Marie MacDonald); for the purposes of the telling, he or she was one of us mortals, which suggests that even the gods have gods. It suggests as well that, for some gods, no one now living is sufficiently Other that a chance encounter with Him or Her in a Hyatt Regency elevator could end up an anecdote over food and wine late in a restaurant in Toronto. One wonders whom Henry Kissinger, say, or Mick Jagger, would consider worthy of bumping into and later telling about, as a story, to his friends. No less than Jesus Christ, probably, or Shakespeare or Napoleon, would do. It *must* be lonely at the top, if you can't even drop names without somehow diminishing yourself.

Later, it occurred to us that a book of brushes with greatness (as it were) could be interesting and, regarding fame and our relation to it, possibly even instructive; it might also be amusing; perhaps downright funny. And, like some of the stories that night over dinner, touching, too. So we put out a sort of cattle-call, soliciting submissions by word-of-mouth and later by a handbill that we mailed to friends, tacked up in laundromats and posted on co-op bulletin boards. And before long, the stories started coming in. A couple of periodicals and radio interviewers picked up on the project and broadcast our solicitation, and soon we were inundated, from Canada, the United States and Britain, from poets, documentary filmmakers, florists and supermarket cashiers. We laid down a few formal restrictions: we asked for short accounts (1-2 book pages) of meetings with 'the giants of our time,' by which we meant people

13

who 'seemed larger than life in the context of your brief meeting.' 'If it happened to you and it took less than ten minutes,' the handout said, 'we want to hear about it!' Everyone who submitted a manuscript understood exactly the kind of encounter we were talking about; no one confused it with a *Reader's Digest* 'Most Fascinating Person' anecdote. This anthology was to be about Fame, and I suppose it is in the nature of Fame that no one misunderstands what is meant by the term. It's what Mother Theresa shares with Howard Cosell.

The variety of voices we heard in these accounts, the range of 'styles,' was pleasing. And revealing, as style always is. Professional writers and people with public lives, like actors, clerics, professors, etc., seemed to have the most trouble coming up with a coherent, unwavering, authentic voice, suggesting, perhaps, their own ambivalent relation to fame. In general, the less sophisticated, less self-conscious writers produced the best writing. They told it straight, because they felt it straight – usually outright adoration, wonder and, relative to the brushee, utter insignificance, which is how one ought to feel in the presence of a deity. (It's probably how one ought to feel when writing.) But for many, the invitation to tell about their meeting with a famous person was an irresistible challenge to their egoism, and the difficulty of meeting that challenge was often betrayed by a stammering, hesitant, over-elaborate voice, mandarin complexity of form, frequent asides and digressions and, in the end, obscurity. The tension between disclosure and withholding was for some writers simply too strong to overcome, and consequently, they wrote awkwardly. Even so, given the thing written about and the occasion of the writing, we felt that frequently the bad writing was as instructive and amusing as the good, and so we did not discriminate against it. As the novelist John Berger says, 'The act of writing is nothing except the act of approaching the experience written about.' But the truth we were after here was not merely the 'experience written about'; we wanted also to examine the brush story itself, as pure behaviour. We wanted to watch it dramatize the conflict between memory and self-creation, between revelation and self-censorship, between history and fiction. We were interested in the morality of rhetoric, as it turned out, and these stories, in a most pleasant way, have given us much to think about.

A few general observations. The narrator / writers of these tales tend to present themselves, regardless of their age at the time of the 'brush,' as child-like or adolescent, emotionally turbulent and confused, weak. Often, relative to the brushee, they are physically small. The brushee, in contrast, is usually large, strong, clear and, perhaps predictably, enigmatic (one might say Delphic). It's interesting to note that frequently the supplicant offers a small gift, with a token / talisman returned, an autograph, a photograph, a validating emblem treasured for years afterward. (See, for example, Mary M. Truitt's encounter with John Lennon, or Charles Wilkins' meeting with Edward G. Robinson.)

The formalist can discern at least six overlapping types, or sub-genres, in the genre, that one might regard as kinds of primal scenes. There is The Meeting with the Great Mother / Father, who offers unqualified love, as in Annie Dillard's awkward dinner with Buckminster Fuller. There is The Permission-Granting story ('Go, my child, and do likewise'), as in Katharine Fehl's account of her meeting with Tennessee Williams. I've already mentioned The Sex God(dess) Validates the Brusher's Sexual Powers story, but a variant, equally popular among male devotees, is The Warrior Approval / Disapproval Encounter, in which the brushee is usually an athlete and the brusher a small boy or adolescent. (See Paul Auster's unprepared meeting with Willie Mays and Martin Chase's Ernest Hemingway story.) Then there is the Even the Gods Die story, in which the brusher discovers mortality, as in R. Gillespie's encounter with the ex-astronaut Neil Armstrong and David Halliday's meeting with an aged Cisco Kid. And finally there is what I call The Transcendent Flash story, as in all meetings with the Dalai Lama (or so it would seem from the submissions) and Joyce Carol Oates' story of meeting Mohammed Ali: in these accounts the devotee experiences hot flashes, anxiety, followed by feelings of inner peace, and then uncontrolled weeping; the brushee usually says and does nothing. No doubt, readers will find other types and sub-genres of their own, but these few seemed to us obvious and of some interest.

It might be helpful to know what we learned about the habitats of the famous, where they seem to hang out. A large number of the encounters reported to us took place in public urinals, elevators and stairwells – urban spaces difficult to avoid, even by those who move about in limousines. There were a large number of restaurant- sightings, which is no surprise, since even the gods eat out, probably more often than the rest of us. Naturally, New York City's Upper West Side weighed in with the most brushes, but for no clear reason there was a relatively large number of sightings in the interior of British Columbia and the northwestern United States, which may say more about the economics of Hollywood movie-making than anything else.

Finally, we would like to thank the hundreds of individuals who submitted stories that, for reasons of space or because they so closely resembled other accounts, we could not include in this anthology. Also, our apologies to those who submitted their brushes too late to meet our publisher's deadline. We hope they will keep an eye out for announcements of *More Brushes with Greatness* and will give us a second chance to consider them for inclusion. To those of you who, unfortunately, have never had a Brush with Greatness, all we can say is: Pray sincerely, and hang out a lot in public restrooms and the woods of British Columbia.

Henry Miller

Philip Willey, Victoria, British Columbia

It was an open-air coffee house in Syntagma Square, Athens. Henry Miller was wearing dark glasses and trying hard to look like any other tourist but I knew it was him all right. He was there every day and I'd been tipped off by people who recognized him for sure. I even had a little opening gambit prepared. It was to be the direct approach again but this time there was to be no hesitation. I sauntered casually over and said, 'Mr. Miller, I....'

'Fuck off,' he said.

I wasn't too upset by the rebuttal. I'd at least tried and he probably saved me the trouble of making a fool of myself, but it did cause me to question the effectiveness of the direct approach. Obviously merely wanting to meet certain famous people was not enough. One had to have an ulterior motive, a subtle *raison*, something with which to elevate oneself, as it were, above simple sycophancy. There had either to be a semblance of equal standing with the subject or else a pretext for the initial contact. Interviews were good for getting round the problem but that discovery was still some way in the future.

Gregor Piatagorsky

Ram Dass, Cohasset, Massachusets

When I was about eleven I went to hear the cellist Gregor Piatagorsky play with the Boston Symphony Orchestra. I was a young aspiring cellist and he, along with Feuerman, who had recently died, were my idols.

After the concert I went backstage. He was surrounded by intense people all speaking Russian. After some time he noticed me and offered me his huge hand to shake. He was about six-foot-four. I had been trying desperately to think of something clever to say. When everyone looked at me, I blurted out: 'I heard Piatagorsky before he died.'

There was a long silence and then Piatagorsky roared with laughter. 'It was Feuerman who died,' he said. 'Piatagorsky is still very much alive.' I was mortified and beat a hasty retreat.

Some years later my uncle met Piatagorsky and reminded him of the incident. Piatagorsky remembered and sent me a note: 'Piatagorsky is still very much alive.'

It is now many years since Piatagorsky died. I heard him before he died.

Colonel Sanders

Gary R. Edwards, Toronto

It was Halifax in the early sixties and my dad's Town and Country Restaurant sold more of the Colonel's greasy bird than any other outlet, so the Colonel himself would come out to pay his respects to this far northeast corner of the New World.

The Colonel was a simple man, a religious man, a family man. And he seemed to like my hard-working father with his house packed to the rafters with seven kids and a pair of country-girl housekeepers, Ethel and Iris. The Colonel preferred our crowded home to the lonely confines of the downtown hotels.

By this time the Colonel was dressing exclusively in his white linen suit with black string tie. For breakfast he ate two boiled eggs and toast. He liked the eggs runny and the toast burnt black. This influenced us kids a great deal and we were thereafter always conscious not to throw away a perfectly decent piece of bread just because it was burnt to a crisp.

Yes, we loved the Colonel. And he touched our lives in many ways. We had a white toy poodle with his face crafted into the colonel's trademark moustache and goatee. Dog's name? Colonel, of course.

In those days before the arrival of the current red-and-white stripe motif, the corporate colour of the Kentucky Fried Chicken franchisee was salmon pink. My dad's 1961 Lincoln Continental was finished in this shade, as was the family boat, an old Cape Island fishing craft built over for cruising. Boat's name? The Lady Colonel, of course. There were even thoughts of dyeing the dog pink during this frenzy of corporate loyalty but my sister Sylvia wouldn't permit it.

In our family KFC was like a religion, with the colonel given the role of God. Even now, as I write this, I worry that I may be committing blasphemy. The old Colonel even looked God-like to us kids. We had God coming to stay with us. Where would he sleep?

My brother David and I were the youngest. We shared a room and it was arranged that the Colonel would be bunking down with us. We assumed that David and I would be forced to share one of the two small beds, leaving the other free for the Colonel. But the

Colonel didn't want to put anyone out of their bed, so he chose to join me, the smallest, in my bed.

I'm not sure if the Colonel knew at the time that I was a notorious bed-wetter. I was five and barely a night passed when I didn't pass my water nocturnally. Mom forbade me from enjoying my evening glass of 7-Up and insisted I use the toilet twice before I skulked off to bed to await His arrival.

While waiting I had a dream. In the dream, I'm struck with the urge to urinate. I head for the washroom, pull my pajama bottoms down around my knees, take careful aim into the bowl and let go. Then I wake up. But there is no toilet, just the Colonel and me curled up in my tiny bed. My pajama bottoms are still up around my waist but they are warm and wet and gradually becoming cold and wet. I close my eyes and head back to sleep, hoping no one will notice.

The Colonel was a good and kind man, a man of high moral standards, but also a man with a sense of humour. And despite his purported senility towards the end of his life he retained a good memory. In 1972, when I was fourteen, he returned to Halifax to appear as the Grand Marshall of the Natal Day Parade in our sister city, Dartmouth. He came with my dad to visit our original outlet on Quinpool Road where I was working after school as a chicken cook. When the Colonel saw me a glint of recognition fell over his bespectacled octogenarian eyes.

'Aren't you the young whippersnapper who pissed all over my leg?' he said.

Barry Morse

Marlene P. McLarty, Prince George, British Columbia

When I heard of your request for brushes with famous people, I thought: 'I've never met, by accident or otherwise, anyone famous.' Then it came flooding back.

In the late seventies a film was being shot at Wells, in the Cariboo Region of British Columbia. The film was *Klondike Fever,* which came out in 1980. A dog-sled scene was being filmed on Jack O'Clubs Lake, and a primary character in the dog-sled scene is the celebrity I was fortunate enough to meet.

Quesnel is about sixty miles from Wells and being a larger town it offers a greater selection of accommodation. I was working at the Quesnel Library at the time and was delighted and thrilled to see Barry Morse enter. He approached the desk in such a friendly manner I lost any shyness I might have felt, and following a long conversation I directed him to the book section of interest to him.

He was interested in the history and geography of the area. In our conversation I mentioned that the Fraser River was just blocks away, Quesnel being situated on the fork of the Quesnel and Fraser rivers.

Prior to his visit to the area, Mr. Morse had been on a TV program in which an astrologist, a palmist and a mind-reader would try to identify the hidden celebrity. During the show he had been told he would soon be visiting the Fraser River, to which he replied: 'Impossible!' He was therefore so surprised to now find himself staying in a motel within blocks of the Fraser.

Other patrons in the library were hesitant to approach him but found him to be such a friendly man they quite enjoyed a brief conversation with him. A thrill for us all.

For years I have been tempted to write 'Thrill of a Lifetime' to request a reunion with this gentleman. I am presently in the throes of self-publishing an illustrated children's book which features my own calligraphy. I guess getting the book launched will be my 'thrill of a lifetime.'

Ezra Pound

Sparling Mills, Halifax, Nova Scotia

In May, 1971, we arrived in Venice and booked into a charming and inexpensive pensione called the Cici. On the walls were pictures of Ezra Pound and handwritten poems signed by him. I was amazed and excited. Obviously we had landed in a special place.

But the woman at the desk spoke no English. She just smiled and nodded when I asked about Pound. A few days later when Wallace and I were walking through the labyrinth of little rooms to the attached restaurant at the back we came upon Pound sitting at a small table with a handsome woman companion, much younger than he. The setting was perfect: dove-grey walls translucent with indirect lighting. I stopped abruptly and he looked up. He must have realized I recognized him and that I was pleased. He nodded slightly, and so did I. But I did not speak.

After that I saw him several more times in the same place with the same woman. Each time Pound would give me a nod. Then one morning about 10:30 we met at the front door, he coming out, I going in. Peggy, my little fox terrier, was with me.

'American?' he asked belligerently.

'Canadian.'

'Ahh,' he breathed, relaxing. He was moving away, when he looked down and seemed to see Peggy for the first time. 'Dogs have to wear muzzles in Venice,' he said gruffly, almost inaudibly.

I tried to look serious. I told him she had one but she wanted to bark at the waves at the Punta della Dogana, hooked her front paw around the muzzle and ripped it off before we could grab it. It fell into the canal.

Pound's frail body shook with laughter. 'She's got spirit, I like that.' Then he turned, and with seemingly infinite concentration, slowly walked to the little bridge and over.

I didn't see him again. We had to leave Venice the next day. A few weeks later I heard he had died.

Veronica Bennett & the Ronettes

Peter Thompson, Vancouver, British Columbia

It was the last weekend of summer before the last year of high school. Curt and I had spent most of that summer cruising in his parents' Chevy II Nova, probably the lowest-status vehicle in Flint, Michigan, home of several GM plants and good deals on Corvettes.

Neither of us had a great love-life and we liked the same music, so aimless drives in the Nova listening to the now-classic songs of the summer of '63 seemed as good a way as any to pass the time.

Because it was early in the evening we heard the announcement on WAMM; they were the black station that signed off at sunset and had a DJ named Bob B. Cue. The Ronettes were performing one night only – that night! – at the equivalent of a Legion hall in the suburbs.

The Ronettes had a hit on the radio at the time, a song that features the most distinctive drum intro in history. It was included in one of those time capsules that the U.S. government buries every year. In an example of uncharacteristic taste, the 1963 capsule contains a copy of 'Be My Baby,' complete with a plaque labelling it 'An Example of the Perfect Pop Record.'

The hall was concrete inside and out. There was no stage and the hundred other kids who were shuffling listlessly to some pretty limp records didn't fill up half the room. We didn't know anyone and it looked like a waste of $1.50.

Then we heard sounds approximating a rock 'n' roll fanfare and someone announced the group. And there they were, looking as erotic and otherworldly as we'd imagined: impossibly long hair, teased way up and falling way down, tight slit skirts, heavy-duty eye-makeup and heavy-hooded expressions, some amazing combination of African, Asian and Mediterranean backgrounds ... they sure knew how to get to the seventeen-year-old boys. We surrounded the trio and gave them some room to move as they wailed away to a prerecorded band track. Curt and I became separated as everyone tried to get a good ogling spot.

As the opening of 'Be My Baby' blasted out – the tape had been edited so that the eight-note Dum-Da-Dum-BAM-Dum-Da-Dum-BAM intro repeated several times – the three Ronettes began walking towards the circle of kids. Veronica (later known as Ronnie, still later as Mrs. Phil Spector) reached out and grabbed my hand and I didn't have a clue what was happening, but I wound up dancing with her for the first part of the song and looked up from my reverie at one point to see Curt dancing with another Ronette. I'm sure my grin was as demented as his and I know neither of us remember a thing about the rest of the band-less performance given that night. But I remain honoured that Veronica Bennett, lead singer of the Ronettes, was the first woman ever to ask me to dance.

Jorge Luis Borges

Edmund White, Paris

I once played host to Borges in New York. It was towards the end of his life when he was willing to go anywhere if he was well paid and provided with first-class air tickets from Buenos Aires for himself and his young companion Maria Kodama (later his wife). He gave the same two speeches everywhere, year after year. I think we had the one about why clichés ('the river of time,' 'the dream of life') make the best metaphors since they contain all the world's wisdom. He granted the same interviews in every town and made the same witticisms at every dinner table, and everyone was always ravished. After he left us he went to Cornell's conference on Nabokov where he cheerfully confessed he'd never read Nabokov but would be happy to give his cliché speech. Everyone was ravished.

I suppose he was a bit like Segovia, similarly old and blind, someone who played the same tunes over and over, an ancient if evergreen repertoire. Although Borges continued to write, all of the stories people admired had been published in the thirties and forties. The elegantly elliptical Borges of that early period, not the more ordinary writer of the sixties and seventies, was the one people wanted. People longed to hear from the librarian to the cosmos about his English-speaking grandmother, his taste for silver-age authors such as Robert Louis Stevenson and G. K. Chesterton, his paradoxes about time and his riddles about reality and fiction. Nobly obliging, Borges was content to play the courtly sham or shaman; he could just as well have sent in his place a polite automaton in a dark suit and a beige vest.

The second night that Borges was installed in the Fifth Avenue apartment I'd found for him, I received a call from Maria Kodama. 'Who is going to wash out Borges' underwear?' she asked. It was a Saturday night and the maid wasn't due to come in again till Monday morning. I thought of doing the job myself but feared embarrassing everyone. I almost asked Maria why she couldn't do it herself. After some discussion we decided that a private maid should be hired first thing Sunday morning and dispatched to solve the problem of the great man's 'Luxables,' as they used to be called.

A hundred bucks to wash out two pairs of scanties at emergency rates. But the odd thing was to think at all of this man's body, he whom Luisa Valenzuela has pictured as an eternal infant who never chose to give in to adulthood.

His lecture drew an overflow audience; the sound of his voice had to be piped out to the hushed students reverently gathered in the lobby and on the stairs. Later, a dinner in his honour was given at a luxurious foundation in a Park Avenue mansion. Maria insisted I sit next to the master. I was intimidated. What would I say?

He asked me to tell him all the latest dirty words in American. As our neighbours with their diamond clips and upswept streaked hair leaned smilingly closer to hear our whispered conversation, a stream of filth poured out of my mouth and Borges nodded, amused. Then he told me why Spanish is not a good language for poetry (the rhyme sounds are all the stock endings of words – sola*mente*, liber*tad* – which are emphatic and lack charm). Beaming and nodding blindly, he confided in me his recollections of his grandmother and his opinions of G.K. Chesterton. I was ravished.

The Cisco Kid

David Halliday, Islington, Ontario

It was the late 1950s. My class had taken a trip to the fall fair at the Canadian National Exhibition grounds. While we were there the word went out that the Cisco Kid was going to appear. The Cisco Kid was one of the many western series that were shown on Saturday morning television. This series starred two Mexicans as good guys who came to the rescue of poor souls, mostly Americans, in the wild west. The hero, the Cisco Kid, a Rudolph Valentino look-alike, always dressed in a black outfit trimmed with silver spangles. He always wore a black sombrero and packed two silver guns. His partner was a good-natured, fat, jovial fellow called Pancho. The two seemed the best of friends, a friendship which was for a young boy as appealing as their good deeds.

A crowd of kids gathered to see the pair. Then they arrived. Or at least the Cisco Kid did. Pancho was nowhere in sight. And though Cisco was dressed in his cowboy outfit this did not allay the disappointment of the kids. They began to chant: We want Pancho! We want Pancho! As the chants grew in volume so did the impatience and then the anger of the Cisco Kid.

I was at the back of the crowd barely able to see much of what was going on. I had two main characteristics as a young boy, a great mop of flaming red hair and shyness. It was the shyness that kept me at the back of the crowd.

Suddenly I saw the Cisco Kid break through the crowd of kids. He was making his way towards me. At first I couldn't believe it. Why me? I wasn't even one of those who had been chanting. Later on I suspected that it was my red hair that had made me a target of the Kid's wrath.

On television the Cisco Kid appeared to have a smooth angelic face, bright round eyes and perfect white teeth. And at a distance he fit this description. But, as he approached me the Cisco Kid began to age. I wanted to turn and run but I couldn't take my eyes off him. The Kid's face was withering, lines began to run across it, circling his eyes, around and into his mouth. His ears were too long, his eyes yellow and sallow. There were bags under his eyes; his teeth though perfectly shaped were yellow.

The Cisco Kid stopped in front of me. His face was flushed. He grabbed me by the collar of my jacket.

'Why do you treat me like this?' he cried. 'I come here for you kids.'

I didn't reply. I just stared at him. He was so wrinkled, so ugly; his breath was awful, smelling like sour milk; he was wearing a wig; he looked so old.

He tried to lift me up.

'Why?' he pleaded.

I wanted to ask him where Pancho was. I looked into the old man's eyes. I didn't have to ask. I knew where Pancho was.

Buckminster Fuller

Annie Dillard, Middletown, Connecticut

I was in my twenties when Buckminster Fuller sat on me. It was 1975. We were having a late dinner in Washington, D.C., following a reception for us at the Folger Shakespeare Library.

The restaurant was dark. Buckminster Fuller was, at best, almost blind and mostly deaf. After dessert he rose and wandered off. I slid into his chair in order to talk to our host and mutual friend, O. B. Hardison. When at length the great man hazarded back to our table, he sat on me, decisively. Only at length, it seemed to me, did he discover what the trouble was.

Bucky – as he signed his subsequent scores of incomprehensible letters – was a great flirt. I didn't grasp this at the time. I thought he liked me. I've never determined if he sat on me by accident. After all, earlier in the evening he had brought his head close to mine and murmured, 'You're very ... universe.'

Bill Kenny of the Ink Spots

Keath Fraser, Vancouver

We were set upon at the second hole by a cigar-smoking black man who declined our invitation to play through and asked instead to join us in an illegal fivesome, and then, talking and swinging so sweetly through the next seventeen holes, had each of us imagining he too, with practice and an acquired rhythm, could some day learn to be cool. Maybe it emerged on the long downhill thirteenth that this interloper had a four-octave range. We were too busy looking in the trees for balls to be anything but blasé. His casual egoism was contagious.

I was thinking of him again recently, watching a perfume commercial that steals one of his songs. *I don't want to set the world on fire ... I just want to start ... a flame in your heart.*

The susceptibility of adolescence was obvious. Touch us with a pro athlete or a pop singer and, bingo, we were checking his card for the straight row to greatness. I date the bouffant F of my signature from the day in grade 10 I got Willie Flemming, the great B.C. Lions halfback, to autograph my briefcase. The briefcase is gone, the sweater I bought from his clothing store on Granville is gone, but the F this man gave me is still in my keeping.

But *combine* sport and music in someone famous and we were talking greatness of another order. By this standard that black man on the golf course turned out to be, well, great. 'He was really great,' we told each other afterwards drinking 7-Up in the clubhouse. His golf we meant; his entertaining non-stop talk; his bustling black soul.

I for one had heard of Bill Kenny and the Ink Spots, probably from listening to Jack Cullen on CKNW, with music from the thirties and forties on his 'Owl Prowl' show. As teenagers, slow-dancing around some dark rumpus room to songs by the Platters, who were we to know, or care, that their sound was heavily in hock to a much earlier group, and in particular to the man now swinging down these fairways with us? He let us know. Not just songs like 'My Prayer' and 'If I Didn't Care' – but the whole style of the Spots, he claimed, had been stolen. There were ten, twenty groups now calling themselves the Original Ink Spots. The real originals hadn't managed to copyright their own ingenuity.

He laughed outrageously at himself, as nimble as any performer on stage. He smoked a cigar a hole and stroking his ball, whether from a scrubby rubber mat or the fairway, with a three-wood or a five-iron, sent it arcing octaves above our own skulled balls that skittered to the forest's edge and beyond. With every shot his left side moved smoothly through the ball, his head motionless, then that right toe pointing to earth again as his hands followed through to sky. 'Go, baby! Up, up! Atta girl! Ha, ha! God love ya, baby!' He'd kiss his iron. And once more retrieve his burning cigar from the fairway and go on with his monologue – interrupting himself only to watch one of us line up another slice, and perhaps to comment on the sheer torque of his swing. 'God bless it!' He admitted to a five handicap, as close to scratch in a golfer as we'd ever seen, let alone played with.

He was semi-retired here in Vancouver. 'It's the only place,' he said. 'The most beautiful city in the world.' He also toured Asia and Europe six months a year, and, apart from performing, his passion was golf. But his golf was a performance too. It strikes me now that his amazing outgoingness and self-possession, not to mention skill and name, weren't enough to get him into one of the private golf clubs along Marine Drive. He was black. And so he played the city's public courses, including this parched one called University, and had probably picked up hundreds of games since moving here with his wife from New York. He played every day. That day, laughing at us all together, 'God love ya!' he kept saying, as if grateful for the chance to tag along. 'They love me in Japan, let me tell you guys, those lovely nips call yours truly the Golden Voice!' His delicate wedge shot at fifteen covered the pin.

At times the Golden Voice would suddenly burst out in a snippet of song to punctuate his running commentary on every subject we could imagine, and more. His talk was a kind of endless song about religion, hypocrisy, echo chambers, show business, smoking, people who had cheated him, delighted him, TV, Brenda Lee, bigots, the Mills Brothers, and drinking. He didn't drink, but he made his own Popsicles. His great love was ballads. 'You know – "We Three," "You Always Hurt the One You Love," "Whispering Grass" – the songs that made us the Spots! We sold millions, honey, round the world. *Today*, if a group sells one hundred thousand they call it a smash hit! You hear what I'm saying?'

We were fuzzy on most of his songs, but it didn't matter. He'd made records. He swung his sticks like a wizard. He waltzed into his own regard with the pitch of personality. We'd never seen anybody like him, always on. His body relaxed when he talked and his pink palms insinuated themselves into the humid air like doves. Swooping down each fairway in huge white shoes, he clearly had his stage. 'I love kids. But I can't stand punks.' We were glad. We were bad, but we weren't punks.

On the sixteenth green he stopped by the flag to tap his forehead. 'Some folks reach me up here,' he told us, and placing his cap over his heart went on, 'but it's the ones who reach me here who count. And I can tell which are which pretty fast....' He studied us – in his late forties and already balding. 'You guys reach me here!' The gesture, the whole hammy salute as he putted out, encouraged affection. 'The same thing applies to singing,' he said, straightening up to full height. 'Unless it comes from down here, in the heart, you're nowhere.'

He enunciated as clearly in person as on record. He would whisper on the tee, imitate this or that celebrity swinging a driver, mention that so-and-so preferred young boys, shake his finger in parody of his mother. Born a twin in Philadelphia and raised a Catholic, he now believed, not in heaven and hell, but in reincarnation. 'If a guy's a cripple, man, could be he's getting punished for something evil in an earlier life. Ha, ha, ha! Bless him!' Rich laughter, subtle prejudice, smooth click of his number-four wood meeting ball as though prearranged. 'Baby, in a man's life there's two things important. You hear what I'm saying? Destiny and Time. If you're destined to do something, you'll do it. The rest is just a question of time.'

Years later I read that this last of the original Ink Spots had discovered he had myasthenia gravis only after falling down on a golf course. When he eventually died it was of respiratory failure, an odd or else fitting death for a tenor of four octaves and 250 recordings. Honoured for his work with foster kids and charities, he was also the author of a book of inspirational poems. 'I'm more proud of that book than if I'd done ten "If I Didn't Cares" or "Whispering Grasses,"' he said.

I like to remember him coming off the seventeenth green talking about the customs officer he'd chatted up a month ago at the Canadian border, who had shown him some impounded pornographic photographs. Puffing a fresh cigar from his last package, Kenny broke into a wide smile, studying us as he described the photo of a nude lady that had caught his imagination. 'Man, should've seen her sitting up there on that stool, her little black box just smiling out at me like somethin' weedy from Leave It to Beaver! Wheeee!' The world was his stage and he saw life's best things as resident upon it. In his vulgarity lay the seal of approval for boys like us, as he knew it did. 'You guys with your hot hands on the pussy! God love ya!'

Then smack went his six iron off the tee, his ball most likely landing in the centre of the eighteenth green, for in those years, before the course was redesigned, it was an elevated green we finally aspired to, making it impossible from the mat to see where a ball might drop should one of us get lucky and fade in a high, elegant shot at the close. We bussed our irons like clowns, and then we struck.

Neil Armstrong

Robert Gillespie, Sherwood Park, Alberta

I was attending a conference in Toronto on the subject of detecting leaks in underground tanks. To my surprise I discovered that Neil Armstrong was one of the scheduled speakers. Apparently one of the business interests of the retired astronaut was in a small company marketing a leak detector. I wondered as I took my seat in the large meeting room in the hotel whether I would actually get the chance to speak to him. What would one say to the first man to walk on the moon? Surely the first person to set foot on a celestial body other than earth would be remembered in human history along with Julius Caesar, Napoleon and Christopher Columbus. It seemed like a link with immortality and a far cry from my average life.

The morning passed and finally Mr. Armstrong and his business partner gave a fairly nondescript presentation. From the back of the room where I was sitting I could barely make out my hero's features.

After lunch some business associates and I were standing in one of the rooms chatting when Mr. Armstrong came and stood in the doorway.

I furtively glanced across in his direction trying to act normal, while my heart was pounding a mile a minute. Should I go and speak to him? I wanted to say thanks for the risks he took that showed us what the possibilities could be. But I also remembered reading an article in *Life* that said he had become a bit of a recluse on his farm because of all the demands for public appearances and interviews. I stood transfixed with indecision. It seemed silly, small and an invasion of his privacy just to go and ask for his autograph. I think I wasn't the only one in the room who had similar thoughts. Everyone continued to chat and study the exhibits while one of the greatest persons in history stood less than fifteen feet away.

Then the strangest thought struck me. He was shorter than I am. I was thunderstruck. Moving a little so that I could look in his direction without turning my head I noticed how very human and vulnerable he looked. His complexion was sunburned and healthy while his face and body were distinctively chubby. He seemed a little uncertain as he stood there alone in the doorway as if he needed a friend. Turning quickly, he left our area and I didn't see him again.

Edward Fitzgerald

Margaret Jane Perfect, Doveton, Australia

It was January 1941, and I was travelling from London to Belfast, Northern Ireland. My husband was a navy man stationed aboard H.M.S. *Suffolk,* and I was going to stay with my sister.

Arriving at Euston Station I found the train was packed to the roof! I did manage to get on, but it was hopeless trying to find a seat. I pushed my way along the crowded corridor looking into each compartment until I finally saw a vacant seat and sat down with a sigh of relief.

Looking round the compartment I noticed I was the only female among six army officers, and one civilian. I was sitting opposite him.

Well, in very slow time (owing to there being an air raid) we left London and the guard came in and asked for our tickets. When I showed him mine he said, 'Do you realize that you are in a first-class seat with a third-class ticket?!!' 'Well,' I innocently replied, 'I *had* to sit down as I am pregnant.' He then replied, 'You can stay if you pay the extra fare,' and my answer was 'I'm sorry, I'm broke.' With that the civilian gentleman across from me said, 'Why not let the lady stay? After all, the seat is vacant and if we run into any more air raids we might all have to get out.'

The ruffled guard withdrew!

Well, after that, my knight errant and I chatted away like old friends and the subject of books came up. He asked me had I ever read 'The Rubaiyat of Omar Khayyam.' I had to confess ignorance and he then said that he had translated it into English and that his name was Lord Donegal.

Well, in due course we reached the end of the journey and said good-bye. With all that was going on in my life I never had the time to read. But many years later I did read 'The Rubaiyat,' and noticed that the translation was by an Edward Fitzgerald. I've often wondered: Was Lord Donegal *the* Edward Fitzgerald, or was I having my leg pulled?

Desmond Tutu
Paul Davidson, Kingston, Ontario

The day I left South Africa – the last Sunday of Advent in 1985 – I attended a very special church service. It was the service to ordain new ministers into the Anglican Church of South Africa. The service was held at St. Mary's Cathedral, a multiracial church as grand and ornate as any in Canada, and for that reason hauntingly familiar. The Right Reverend Desmond Tutu led the service.

The service had an inspiring blend of Christian traditions. There was the incense of a high mass, the festive music of Handel, the enthusiasm of an evangelical crusade, and three African choirs singing in rich harmony.

Tutu was resplendent in his red robes, staff and hat. As part of the ordination process, he asked the congregation if we accepted the ordinands as ministers of the church. When we mumbled an affirmative response, Tutu was taken aback and countered in jest, 'Well, do you? These men have studied for years for this day. You can do it better?' This time we got it right and responded with a tumultuous 'Yes!'

When it came time for greeting each other with the peace, I was pleased to see a genuine and enthusiastic exchange between all races. Now in churches at home the peace ranges from an exchange of words, to a handshake, and in some university congregations, a hug. Ministers usually greet people in the first few pews. But at that very special service, Tutu greeted people all the way to the back of the cathedral which held about a thousand. And Tutu greeted the people with powerful embraces.

At a reception for ordinands following the service, Tutu moved through the crowd, greeting each of the ordinands by name, and telling stories about each to their families. He smiled, he joked, he laughed. Throughout this I stood in the background watching and marvelling at his intense humanity. Our eyes met, and he came straight over to meet me. He was smaller than I thought he would be. But his legendary laugh broke my shyness, and soon we were discussing the role of the church in the struggle that was raging just beyond the courtyard. When I told him I was returning to Canada he asked me to pass his greetings on to 'our brothers and sisters' and urged them to continue their prayers for South Africa. The exuberant little man left me, but not before giving me a bear hug that left my ribs aching all the way home to Canada.

Cliff Robertson

Daniel F. Richard, Winnipeg

I was working alone in the Red Wing shoe store in Vancouver, British Columbia, on a Thursday, when I received a phone call from a salesman from another shoe store looking for hunting boots for a customer. After talking to me, he told me that he was sending down a man who needed the boots for a part in a movie he was making in Vancouver. He would be there in about an hour to get fitted. I was not too pleased about this as I would normally be closed and on my way home in an hour, but I was more than a little curious as to whom the customer might be. After all, Vancouver was getting a reputation as being Hollywood North and it could be just about anybody from television or the movies!

An hour went by and no one showed up; and then a grey limousine with smoked-glass windows pulled up in front of the store. Out of it stepped a man that I recognized immediately – Cliff Robertson, a Hollywood actor who won the Oscar for Best Actor for playing Charly in the movie of the same name, and more recently as Hugh Hefner in *Star 80*, the true story of a local B.C. girl, Dorothy Stratton, who grew up a mere five miles from here!

He was in Vancouver to make the movie *Malone* with Burt Reynolds and he had left his own hunting boots at his home in New York. I let him in and locked the door behind him as I was now closed. While I fitted him up with a pair of boots, we talked about his movies and television work and about the new movie, *Malone* (I meant to see it, but I never did).

After he had decided on a pair, he asked me a very unusual question – could I 'distress' the boots (his word for making the boots look well-used) and could I build up the heels about an inch so that he would look larger and be slightly thrown forward? I told him I'd find a way to 'distress' the boots and our shoe-repair service could build up the heels and he could pick them up in a few days.

I asked him for an autograph so he wrote a 'thank you' with his signature on one of my business cards. We shook hands and he disappeared into the limo. It was the first and last time I ever saw him because someone else picked up the boots.

John Lennon

Robert Fones, Toronto

4:00 p.m., Wednesday, June 4, 1969
as recorded in personal journal

Betty called at about 3:00 p.m. and said that she had made a lot of phone calls and found out that Lennon was staying at the Windsor Arms on St. Thomas Street, west of Yonge and Bay. Jim got John's camera and we left to try and find the hotel. Jim bought some film and we walked down Bloor looking for St. Thomas Street. I looked in a store on Bay Street at a Toronto street guide and found that the street was just west of Bay. St. Thomas is only two blocks long and the Windsor Arms is a small five-storey, red-brick hotel with ivy growing all over the front. A limousine was parked out front. Two girls waited by the front door. It was cool and cloudy. We stood across the street for awhile and then went over and asked the girls if they were waiting for John Lennon. They said they were. Nobody else seemed to know about it. A few people came in and out of the front door. John asked the limousine driver if he was Lennon's chauffeur. He said, 'No, I'm Mr. Grace's chauffeur.' Then he got out of the car and we all started firing questions at him. I felt sure he was putting us on. I went to a phone booth and called the hotel and asked for Mr. Lennon. The receptionist rang his room and then told me there was no answer. 'When will he be back?' I asked. She said she didn't know. I went back to the hotel. The girls had gone inside. We stood outside because they wouldn't let anyone else inside. A few young guys with cameras and pads went inside. I asked a guy with fuzzy hair what was up. 'Is John in there?' 'Yes, but we don't want anyone to know,' he said quietly. 'That's why he's staying here.' Another limousine drove up. Some people who looked like part of the Lennon entourage stood around outside and inside. I was shaking. I was so goddamn nervous. I couldn't believe that John Lennon was really inside the building. A man inside said he would be coming down in a few minutes. John Misczcyk and I were going nuts. Jim was excited I guess but not as much as John and I. The atmosphere was getting very tense. Then the doors opened. An older man with grey hair came out followed by the fuzzy-headed guy. I heard some talking inside. A girl said, 'Could I have your autograph?' Then out came John Lennon. I almost died. I handed him the envelope with five Blanky buttons, five checkerboard buttons and the Blanky Story in it saying, 'Here's something for you, John.' 'Oh, thanks very much!' he said. Then I said, 'Could I have your autograph?' 'Yeah, sure,' he replied. I gave him my pen and he wrote his name in the back of my book. I watched amazed as he wrote it. He handed it back to me. Then I saw Yoko and Kyoto. They were all in black. Lennon had on a black turtleneck sweater, black coat and pants. I didn't notice the colour of his shoes. Guys were taking pictures. John and Jim were taking some too. He looked so fantastic. So cool. They all looked beautiful. Yoko and Kyoto got in first and then John got in, sitting on the side nearest me. Jim had the camera now, taking photos through the window. John opened the envelope and took out the buttons and story. He put on a Blanky button and gave one to Yoko. He put one on Kyoto. Then he put on a checkerboard button and started looking at the story. He looked out at me. I was so happy. I just stood there smiling. Then the limousine started to drive away and Lennon made the peace symbol with his hand. Yoko turned around and waved. The limousines drove away. I was stunned. We started to walk away. We were all blubbering and saying, 'Jesus Christ! Oh my god! I don't believe it! Fuck! John! We really saw him! Jesus!' We were all acting stoned. Nothing else mattered. Jim took the film and left for the *Globe and Mail*. John and I raved about it all the way home. We met one of the girls who had been there and she had John's and Yoko's autograph. She said my Lennon autograph was better than hers. How stupid can you get. She should be glad she even saw him. John and I went home and just sat around. We didn't know what to do.

Sonny Bono

Sharon Thesen, Vancouver

I once lived with a man whose ex-wife had had an affair with Sonny Bono.

Marcel Duchamp

Michael Snow, Toronto

Starting around 1948 I became interested in Marcel Duchamp. I liked and studied Matisse, Mondrian and Klee just as much in my 'formative' years and was following closely what was happening in American art. However, Duchamp's work, personality and life became an especially important inspiration. My admiration deepened as I saw and read more and more. It seemed that there wasn't as much information available on his work as on that of certain other artists. He was a special case. Of course he was famous in a rather underground way during the early fifties but though he was often mentioned in the pantheon with Picasso, Matisse, Mondrian, Miro, his name was usually after theirs and others. He wasn't ever regarded as *du champ* (unlike Picasso) but was 'unique,' an odd inventor of his own area of art.

Though he'd been associated with Dada he was different enough from the others to seem to be a movement of one. The work of the artists mentioned above (especially Matisse and Picasso) with its sensuousness and expression reinforced the unique coolness of Duchamp's contribution. But he made it evident that in some ways he had clarified his course 'against' theirs.

Duchamp's aristocratic, hands-clean aloofness was intriguing. His seeming freedom from the excessive demands for ego gratification which appeared to be an aspect of the character of many artists (exemplified by his non-involvement with the art marketplace and its publicity machine) was inspiring. Though Picasso, for example, couldn't exactly be called a 'commercial' artist he certainly did produce a great deal and exhibit constantly. Enough for it to appear a 'product.' Duchamp made little, had very few exhibitions, and the 'ready-mades' critiqued the hand-making of original works for sale. Much of his work, but in particular the 'Large Glass,' had the capacity to arouse a desire to penetrate its secrets. In this sense the viewer of his work resembles the 'outsider' viewer of the arcane texts of secret societies, of alchemists, or the artifacts of a non-Western culture. He made private languages that continue to invite translation.

Abstract Expressionism, house-painterly work that was in many ways antithetical to Duchamp's, took the stage. But soon his work moved a little more into the spotlight, something that disappointed me (!) when in 1958-1960 the work of the younger new American painters Robert Rauschenberg and Jasper Johns started to attract critical attention. He was decidedly an influence on them. John Cage, who had a marginal and legendary reputation similar to that of Duchamp, in my view, in the fifties also seemed to be becoming more appreciated, more generally accepted.

Some of the thinking involved with my 'Walking Woman Works' (1961-1967) had to do with putting art elsewhere, in contexts other than art contexts (galleries, etc.). I reversed the order of an aspect of Duchamp's work. Rather than choosing and taking a 'ready-made' from 'the world' and putting it in an art context, I made a 'sign' from within the art context and put it in the world. I did make lots of gallery work but what was specifically related to Duchamp were what I called 'Lost Works' which existed anywhere but in a gallery (on the street, in stores, in the subway) or in a gallery where I was not exhibiting: in hidden or normally unused places, for example. 'Lost Work' stuck under a bench, a chair, a table of the Green Gallery in 1965. Or as fortuitous-looking ephemera (Museum of Modern Art, New York, 1966). These 'Lost Works' are discussed in Louise Dompierre's text in the catalogue *Walking Woman Works* (1983).

Michel Sanouillet taught at the University of Toronto during the fifties, knew Duchamp, was an expert on him, Picabia and Dada in general. He'd written a book on Duchamp which I had. Greg Curnoe knew him too. I never knew him well, but enough for it to feel okay to ask him if he would be kind enough to arrange a meeting for Joyce Wieland and me with Duchamp.

Joyce and I had decided to move to New York and did so in 1963.

'Monsieur Duchamp, my name is Michael Snow. Michel Sanouillet said he would be kind enough to ask you if you would do my wife and me the honour of meeting you.'

Without much ado he chose a time and invited us to his walk-up apartment – on 11th Street near Fifth Avenue, I think it was.

Joyce made a stuffed red heart as a gift for him and I brought some rubber-stamped 'Walking Woman' stickers which I was using for some of the 'Lost Works.'

I was nervous, apprehensive.

Up we go and in we go, meet him and his wife Teeny. Gracious greetings. Interesting apartment. History. Work by Tanguy, Miro, Matisse, Ernst reminded me that during the legendary years when Duchamp had 'given up art for chess' he'd made the occasional dollar by middle-manning the sales of paintings by his famous confreres. My mind sneered: 'He didn't dislike "messy," "sensitive" painting so much that it prevented him from getting his hands dirty with a few filthy bucks. Un-commercial, eh?'

This was the beginning of a descent in the elevator of my psyche direct to the basement.

I felt shitty. The apartment was interesting, yeah, but what the hell, it was really just another New York 'railroad' dump which probably had as many cockroaches as any other.

We sat, watched, listened.

The master seemed to be basking in our adoration a bit too much. Joyce gave him the stuffed red heart. He said, 'Oh, thank you. This reminds me of my "Coeurs volants." I guess you must have been thinking of that. Did you know that if you put together two complementary colours of the same value beside each other they make a kind of optical vibration?'

'Complementary! Maybe he meant complimentary! That was hardly an ego-less remark.' Internally, I snickered. My elevator went to the sub-basement. I was getting angry. 'Who does this guy think I am, talking to me like that! Does he think he's some kind of art-school teacher and we're his students? Of course I knew that!' During our conversation I managed to say something about me. (He didn't seem to give a shit who we were or what we did, just talked about himself.)

I gave him my gift without blurting out any of the above sentiments. I told him that I was making a film (which eventually became *New York Eye and Ear Control*) and would like to shoot a short scene with him in it. He said he would be glad to, which surprised me. But: 'Pretty accessible after all. And maybe he agreed to it because he's just as much of a sponge for attention as all the other artists!'

Far from being ego-less, this guy seemed to love compliments. I became super-critical of everything he said, which echoed against the concrete walls of my sub-basement. 'This guy is supposed to be so witty, well, what a stupid thing he just said. And that superior smile!'

I now wondered if we were part of a parade of admirers! He

wasn't supposed to care about other people caring, but now I thought: 'He doesn't make art anymore, he just sits in here every day soaking up international admiration for what he did do!' He had a small Yves Klein sponge stained International Klein Blue. Probably a gift. Klein had recently died tragically young. Duchamp spoke of him, saying 'He was a beautiful boy.' Snort! Me: 'Sounds like he's gay too! So all that wonderful hetero intellectual smut in his work is just a cover-up. A closet case. He *is* Rose Selavy!'

I got more and more uncomfortable, strangling on my tea ('lousy tea, what the hell are these tasteless biscuits?') until finally we grovelled our way out with me gasping for air (and not 'Air-de-Paris') and Joyce wondering what was wrong. During our descent to the street I was still in my psychological sub-basement, and started to fume through all my negativities, which surprised her.

As I ranted and walked my neurotic elevator started to rise, and I started just slightly to question myself. Joyce listened generously, and fortunately my self-questioning continued as I reached the first floor with the beginnings of embarrassed horror. I gradually realized with deep dismay how far I had sunk under an Oedipal lump which had exceeded the weight limits of my elevator. I don't believe I wanted to marry Teeny but I sure had wanted to kill my Dada.

My poor ego was so frail at that particular time that I was unable to encounter a superior with the respect and curiosity that my psyche felt when all the floors were in contact (or, when I lived on the main floor and disregarded messages from the furnace room?). I'd gone in there on my knees and it hurt.

I'll never forget my self-disgust and amazement at how a 'level' of my mind (to stick with the questionable Freudian architectural divisions) could hysterically take over the supervision of the building and shut off the heat and light on the other floors. I hoped it would never happen again.

Since what I had experienced was exceedingly and no doubt falsely insulting to Duchamp, I felt like apologizing to him. (Didn't. What could he have noticed?) Phoned a week later to ask if we could meet again and shoot the little scene: Joyce and Marcel walking across the street, seen through a mask of the 'Walking Woman' outline.

Unfortunately, I couldn't use this shot in the film. Another story. Brush with money. Still. Later.

At our second meeting I was 'cured.' He was interesting and I was interested; he enjoyed doing the little bit of film and seeing us again. He was an extraordinary man and I regret having wasted an opportunity to know him.

Since that abysmal meeting I've had occasion to recount cathartically my descent, but this is its first appearance in embarrassing print.

Tom Jones

Sonja A. Skarstedt, Montreal

I was fifteen, gawky, acne-plagued. My chief goals were to sing like Judy Garland and to invent a formula that would shrink my five-foot-eight frame down to an appropriately insignificant five-two. I believed that anything was possible, even meeting somebody famous.

Opportunity presented itself in the form of a radio announcement one afternoon: 'Ladies, how would you like to catch Tom Jones' concert at the Place des Arts? How would you like to meet Tom backstage after the show? All you have to do is mail in your name, address and telephone number and – who knows? Maybe you'll be the lucky winner!'

Winning radio contests had become one of my specialties: in the preceding two years I had managed to win everything from grocery samples and dinner-for-four to a Mother's Day hat. So why not Tom Jones?

Actually I was more familiar with Glenn Miller and Fats Waller than Tom Jones. The last time I had seen the performer was back in the sixties, during the heyday of his television show. I was eight, more enthralled by the chorus of neon-caged go-go dancers than the tight-suited, gyrating star they were backing up. I could also recall the screaming all-female audience.

I found a thank-you card in my mother's stationery drawer and inscribed a word balloon on the cover, so that the watercolour frog seemed to exclaim: 'I listen to CJAD!' Inside, I wrote: 'I have always wanted to meet a famous person because I want to be famous when I grow up. There are many questions I would ask Tom Jones if I could meet him in person. And I would love to go to a real show at the Place des Arts.'

I returned home from school one Wednesday afternoon and turned on the radio. 'This is the day, ladies!' chirped Jack Finnigan. 'Later on this afternoon, I'll be announcing the lucky gal who'll get to meet Tom Jones backstage at the Place des Arts!' My stomach prickled in anticipation. No, I shook my head, it's probably rigged....

An hour and a half later I was upstairs in my room, sketching, when I heard my mother shouting my name. 'You've won, Sonja! You've won!' The prickly sensation returned, this time propelling my entire body down the stairs. 'I knew it! I had a feeling I'd win!' I shouted above the elated screams of my mother and brother Stephen.

The telephone started ringing, with numerous women, one of whom had sent in 237 entries, begging me to take them along to the show. 'No,' I stated as determinedly as I could, 'I'm taking my father with me.'

'You're sick!'

This decision to take my father only enhanced my weirdo status at school: 'You *would* take your father to see Tom Jones!' Of course my father did possess a Nikon and a comfortable car.

On Saturday, May 15, I washed my hair and inspected the viscose and polyester jumble of my wardrobe. I decided on a pale-blue short-sleeved gym top and navy slacks, topped off with a camel-coloured woollen jacket and a pair of sneakers. Just be yourself, I thought.

When we arrived at the Place des Arts I found myself surrounded by a sea of pearls, perfect coiffures and evening gowns, the silk-and-sequined cream of Montreal concert-goers. I wished I could dissolve into my off-white sneakers, feeling slightly placated when I remembered that my father was wearing a respectable black business suit.

Jack Finnigan greeted us when we arrived at our reserved seats. I shook his hand, wondering why he somehow didn't fit the image evoked by his radio voice.

'It doesn't look good,' he mumbled. 'Mr. Jones' manager has made it clear they want no shrieking women backstage.'

'But I don't shriek!' My chin felt as if it had tumbled into my stomach. So, this was it. No Tom Jones.

Jack patted my shoulder. 'Look, I'll go back and see what I can do.' He headed backstage and we exchanged hellos with his girlfriend, an affable social worker whose chic haircut and pink-tinted glasses I immediately envied.

Jack returned with a smile. 'I did it! I explained to the manager that you're not the shrieking type, you're a nice, studious girl who wears glasses and came with her father. And he says it's okay!' My elation returned. For once it paid to be the 'studious type.'

We settled back to enjoy the show. A spotlight flashed and out pranced Tom in a lacy white shirt and purple satin suit. Even his patent-leather shoes gleamed. 'Oh my God,' groaned Jack's girlfriend. As the hall reverberated with ecstatic screams I sat there in awe.

After the show we were ushered beyond the forbidden doors leading backstage. As we waited in the hallway a wave of anticipation and disbelief came over me as a mob of photographers and reporters blocked the path. Would I really meet Tom Jones? Would I really have the nerve to ask him any questions?

A PR man slipped an eight-by-ten glossy photo of Tom into my hand: 'You can ask him to sign this!' It was at this moment that Jack's calm affable girlfriend unravelled. She began to sputter, as if her body had been possessed by an earthquake.

'Oh my God! I can't believe it! *Tom Jones!*' Oh blast, I thought, now Tom will never let us in.

'Hey there, Sonja,' teased my father. 'Are you getting a little nervous about meeting old Tom?'

'Of course not, dad!'

'Mr. Jones will see you now!' The harried voice of the PR man was blocked out by my realization that this was it. As we filed down the hall I hoped that Tom wouldn't hear the broken sobs of Jack's girlfriend directly behind me.

The dressing room was bustling with about twenty people performing various tasks: snapping pictures, shouting orders, packing bundles of wire and equipment, bringing boxes of take-out food. Somebody gripped my arm: 'Miss, here's Tom Jones!'

Standing directly in front of me was a tall man wearing a bright red body suit. 'How do you do, miss?' The gravelly greeting came from a ruddy-cheeked face consisting of a warm smile and sparkly-brown eyes, surrounded by a mop of frizzy dark hair. Tom Jones, indeed!

'Would you like me to sign that, then?' He motioned to the photograph in my left hand. My eyes were fixed on the gold crucifix nestled in the hairs of his chest. Even Tom Jones is religious, I thought.

I tried to gather my thoughts against the blaring lights and activity, handing him the photo. 'I guess you get tired of signing these, eh?' The words tumbled out of my mouth at 78 RPMs.

'Nah! It's part of the job, y'know.' I wondered how he could sing so smoothly in spite of such scratchy vocal cords.

'What's it like to be famous?' Ah, the key question.

'It's wonderful. I love it.' He took out his pen.

'Don't you feel nervous going out onstage?' My hands twisted together. How dare I ask such audacious questions?

'You bet! But once I'm up there – I just go! It's a real high!'

'So – you like being famous?'

'Well, the job takes a lot of hard work, but I wouldn't trade it for anything.' The pen was still paused above the photo, ready to sign.

'Hmm.' I didn't dare bother him with further questions. 'That's an elegant suit you're wearing – it'd make a great winter outfit!' I tried to ease my voice into a comfortable, joke-cracking pace.

'Yeah – hah! It's comfortable!' His Welsh accent rather enhanced the 'hah!' I thought. 'So....' He started writing on the photograph. 'Is "Sonja" spelled with a "y" then?'

'No, with a Swedish "j"!' I cracked, spying a box of take-out food on his dressing table. He must have been hungry.

'So, you aren't Russian then?'

'Not yet!' My fingers were still frozen together.

'Now, would you mind if I gave you a kiss?' Tom asked rather eloquently, staring me warmly in the eye. I, being one of those people who rarely, if ever, blushes, could actually feel my cheeks growing warmer. I had forgotten about this part. Of course: Tom Jones, the ladies' man, would insist on giving his lady admirer a kiss.

'Er –' What could I say? 'Yes please!' I could hear my father chuckling away.

Tom leaned over and gave me the second kiss I'd ever received. It was the equivalent of a wet, electric buzz and took about a quarter of a second. What would those girls back in school think? My cheeks felt like two flames. Why did so many people have to watch?

While I stood back smiling a shy, frozen smile, Jack's girlfriend managed to wobble towards Tom. 'Oh my God, Tom! *I love you, Tom!*' she yelped. Her chic, tinted glasses were streaked by tears and her exuberant red face nearly matched the red in Tom's bodysuit.

Tom gripped her shoulders. 'There, there, darling ... relax.' He gave her a hug and kiss. 'You'll be all right.' I spied a hint of consternation in his eyes.

'Mr. Jones, would you mind posing for a photograph?' I looked up in surprise. It was my conservative, business-minded father.

'Certainly, sir!' Jack's girlfriend was leaning against Tom, her eyes resembling two enraptured light bulbs. Jack stood nearby, shaking his head like a defeated salesman. It was then that I particularly appreciated my father's presence. As he snapped his Nikon I loosened up a bit, thinking what a great souvenir this photograph would be. As it turned out, this meeting with Tom Jones would be the last contest I would win for a while. It was, however, the contest to end all contests: I had enjoyed chatting with a famous person and discovered in the process that being famous was simply part of the job, at least as far as Tom Jones was concerned. Onstage, he was the electrifying performer and ladies' man. Offstage, he was another human being doing his job and looking forward to a good meal.

The Dalai Lama

William J. Murphy, Watertown, Maine

I grew up as part of the 'lost generation' of the sixties; I wandered back and forth from coast to coast, from the Cape to the Haight a couple of times, went to Woodstock, watched the whole scene go sour. Then I worked for seven years as a fisherman, mostly in Maine. One winter, having nothing else to do, I enrolled at the little university extension in Machias. They had a degree program there called biological technology, which was supposed to turn clam-diggers like me into concerned bachelors of science. And I did pretty well, at first, until I ran head-on into calculus and chemistry. My grades plummeted, and finally, ignoring my advisers, I decided to change courses: I became a lowly liberal arts major.

That's how I found myself, one Columbus Day weekend, on an art history field trip to the museums in and around Boston. Nearing thirty, I was not only far and away the oldest kid in the class, but I also happened to be the only male in the group; most of the men in northern Maine are not art hounds, I guess. So I was elected chauffeur.

We didn't arrive in the city until late, and most of my class-mates went immediately to bed, but I stayed up for a while to watch the news and hear the baseball scores. What caught my attention, though, was a piece on the Dalai Lama; he was in the States for a visit, and was giving an audience at Harvard University the next day. I told the others about it at breakfast, and they talked about how great it would be if the Dalai Lama were to give an audience at Machias. This not being very likely, I suggested we get started on our rounds.

Late in the afternoon, after a long day of wandering through the halls of the Museum of Fine Arts, I drove the gang over to Cambridge, and eventually, after circling the neighbourhood a couple of times, found a parking spot on a quiet little side street. My friends spread out through the square to do some shopping, but I decided to stay with the car and wait for them. I rolled a cigarette, sat back, and had a look around. I was parked in front of a wrought-iron gate that opened onto a shady courtyard, fronting a large brick cottage with white shutters around the windows, and over the door a brass

53

plaque commemorating something or other. I guessed it was probably a frat house for the sons of millionaires. Suddenly two men were standing next to the car.

'Licence and registration, please!'

'Say what ...? Okay, sure, hold on a second.'

'What are you doing here?'

'Here it is. Who are you guys, anyway? What's going on? Can't you park here?'

The short haircuts, the wary eyes, the tailored steely-blue suits, the general aura of fitness, and, above all, the right hand inside the jacket – these must be some kind of Secret Service men. I knew I was innocent of any major crimes, so I told them the truth: 'I'm sitting here waiting for some friends who went shopping.' And they believed me.

They left, and I lit another cigarette, wondering what the hell was going on. Just then the front door of the cottage opened, and out came more Secret Service men clutching walkie-talkies to their ears. What the hell? Who are all these officials? What are all these guys in orange robes? The Dalai Lama? The goddamn Dalai Lama, the nine-hundredth incarnation of Buddha or something! I climbed out of the car and walked a few steps towards what had suddenly become a small procession: the walkie-talkies, local police, American and Tibetan officials, monks and clergymen, and then, all alone in the calm centre of the public swirl, came the Dalai Lama. He was passing just a few feet from me and suddenly he stopped and turned to me. He looked at me, smiled, bowed slightly, and gave me a friendly little wave. And in that moment something passed between us, some sort of confirmation, like a flash of light, a scent of flowers. I know it sounds sort of pseudo-mystic and Hare Krishna, but something sweet really did wash through me; I started to cry. His entourage hustled him off to a parking lot across the street, and I just stood there, stunned, like Paul on the road to Damascus.

And that's how the Dalai Lama of Tibet and the clamdigger from Maine crossed paths in Boston one day. When the other art enthusiasts returned and asked me what had happened, all I could say was: 'I've been blessed, I've been blessed.' They wanted to know if I could still drive. 'Sure,' I replied. 'Anywhere you want to go.'

Anita O'Day

William Matthews, New York City

In 1957 I stood next to Anita O'Day at a concession stand at the Newport Jazz Festival. She took a first sip of coffee from a paper cup and gave it a glum look. She was dressed like a Laura Ashley wet dream – a floral print dress with a skirt belled enough to swirl and a beribboned straw hat with a vast floppy brim. Due onstage in an hour, she rummaged in her purse for a cigarette. Good God, I thought, it's Anita O'Day, toes and ears and all.

She wore an expression I now recognize from the inside out. There's a cartoon in William Steig's 'Fellow Creatures' that shows a middle-aged man in a sports coat on the balls of his feet, grinning. The caption? 'Professor Greeting New Students with Pleasantries.' And there have been entire literary parties through which I have helplessly carried a look like her's on my face like a cheerful shadow.

'Honey,' she asked, 'have you got a light?' I lit her crumpled cigarette. And then I didn't back away, I didn't say anything, I just stood there. I was fifteen. 'You havin' a good time?' she asked.

It was a smoker's voice, rumbly at the circumference. I was so stunned by the pleasure of the moment that I confessed. 'Right now I am.' Smoke lolled out of her mouth into her nostrils.

She looked at me slant. I didn't understand my feelings, I couldn't name them, but I sure as hell had them and could say so. Maybe she recognized the emotional configuration of a musician, though I was a bad musician in those days and never grew better and gave it up. And I'd had a light.

Whatever it was, it was already done. She gave me a little flounce and tossed her head. 'You'll be all right,' she said.

Katharine Hepburn & Robert Helpmann
Timothy Findley, Cannington, Ontario

In 1954, I was performing in a play called *The Prisoner* at the Globe Theatre in London's West End. My part required a very great number of props, all of which had to be counted over before each performance.

On matinee days, the actors rarely left the theatre between performances because, in England at that time, the curtain came down about 5:30 and went back up at 7:00.

The curtain falls, of course, when a play is over – but soon as the audience has left the theatre, the curtain is raised and a battery of cleaning women comes in to vacuum the aisles and pick up discarded programs. Visiting celebrities very often take advantage of this moment to come up out of the house and reach the stars' dressing rooms simply by crossing the stage instead of going outside and having to face the mob of autograph seekers hanging around the stage door....

So there I was, late on a Wednesday afternoon, standing in the wings counting over my props after the first performance, when I heard somebody coming out of the house and over the footlights, preparing to cross the stage. Of course, I leaned forward to see who it was – and there was Katharine Hepburn and Robert Helpmann.

In those days, Hepburn affected a scarlet opera cloak. Helpmann, for his part, always affected high-heeled shoes – because of his shortness. The image, then, is of two of the greatest stars of all time – suddenly marching into the presence of a traumatized young actor (me) – thinking they could escape unrecognized.

Well – they couldn't.

The scarlet opera cloak swirled into view – with Hepburn's neck and head above it. *Clickety-click, clickety-click* – the high-heeled shoes tipped the image of Robert Helpmann perilously forward in my direction.

I stepped from behind the property table. I don't know what I had in mind. Perhaps I was thinking I might just say 'hello.' But instead, I felt myself floating towards the floor....

Not in a faint. No such luck.

I had curtsied.

And I mean the full court-curtsy of another age, the kind once offered only to the Kings of France.

Miss Hepburn paused and stared and blinked.

Mr. Helpmann was more succinct. Regarding my lowered self, he said: 'Oh no, dear boy – no need! No need!'

And they both swept on.

Jules Léger

Randall Ware, Ottawa, Ontario

It was in the late spring of 1974. Not long before, I had been hired as the first full-time executive director of the Canadian Booksellers Association in order to bring the book retailers more fully into the professional world of writing and publishing in Canada. Part of my responsibility was to represent my members at the various meetings and functions that flourish in this industry. I had received an invitation to attend the Governor General's Awards which were to be given at Rideau Hall in Ottawa. Given that these were the most prestigious literary awards in the country, I felt it my duty to go and demonstrate our interest in such matters.

It was raining in Ottawa when I arrived. I had contacted several local booksellers and asked them to join me in attending the ceremony. Part of the reason for the invitation was to show them that their new director was as comfortable in the sophisticated climate of literary society as he was in discussions of publishers' discounts and return policies.

The taxi delivered us to the front door of the Governor General's residence where we were admitted to the foyer. I recognized a friend on the other side of the room and started across to say hello, removing my damp coat as I went. In the course of my passage across the room, I came upon an elegant gentleman in a morning suit. I asked him if it were possible that he might take my coat. As if by magic, another dark-suited gentleman appeared to take the coat from his hands and removed it to its proper resting place.

I had mistaken the Governor General, Jules Léger ... for a servant.

He, too, was new at his job and handled the situation with dignity. In fact he stayed in his job longer than I stayed in mine, but that's another story.

Norman Mailer

Bob Solomon, Edmonton, Alberta

One day when I was in Lenox, Mass., I received a phone call from a friend's son: 'Mailer's in the Lenox Inn drinking. You've got to meet him and tell him everything.' Billy had heard the Pentagon story by firelight when he was twelve; he knew Mailer from talking with him about *Moby Dick* and *The Naked and the Dead* while showing him around a mansion Mailer had wanted to rent. Billy had listened to my tales of meeting Mary and Bumby Hemingway, and Faulkner's next-door neighbour in Oxford. But now everything was wrong: it was not the time for me to meet a celebrity, not even one I had almost gone to jail with or to battle in front of. I was sick, caught in the iron embrace of asthma after two days in the Berkshires, two nights with Billy's cat. But, head pounding with every breath, I nevertheless worked my way the two miles of country roads into town to peer through the windows of the old brick inn. No Mailer. I walked in. I checked the other pub in vain, looking for a dancing or drinking tough guy. As I retreated, in fresh humiliation, muttering recriminations, I paused to rest my heaving chest against the comforting cool steel of my car's door before lowering myself into the seat. And there he was. Mailer walked across the street ten feet away, his head turned towards me. He could not have missed my uneven steps and loud, gasping breaths. He approached, and a streetfighter's eyes met mine.

'Goddamn. Norman Mailer,' I choked out ... and could not breathe to finish. Mailer stopped. He looked up and offered a warm and soft open right hand, and then with a cat's ease he pointed the thumb of his other hand towards a dark-haired, slim companion, a woman who was staring anxiously at my tall, wheezing figure in the yellow dazzle of the streetlights. 'This is my wife, Carolyn.' She came back, perhaps relieved at not being in a Mailer battle with a challenging stranger, a common expense of loving her man. I spoke in halting phrases of who I was, where I worked. 'I've taught all your books,' I said to Mailer. Every time my hoarse voice died to a croak, Carolyn blanched and started. But Mailer looked at me with a sadness and softness that ended my search for words and armoured Carolyn and him against any threats that night. There was no air to tell him of my awfully respectable but scared initiation into the anti-war crowd seven years before. My lungs burned and my bronchi screamed for attention. The moment with all I had wanted from it, slipped, like the cool night air, between my fingers and was gone. Mailer left in his silver Porsche, Carolyn in a silver Audi, racing after each other down the empty country road. I drove homeward, thinking that I had spent too many years fighting my body, and wondering what demon of mind or gland decreed flight or silence for me, and why. At that moment getting home at once, to my medicine, meant more than telling Mailer that once upon a time I had felt all that he had afterward written, that with a raincoat on one arm and a girl whose name I had forgotten on the other, I learned all that he felt and put onto paper in *The Armies of the Night*, some of it, anyway. Rasping the mountain air into my heaving chest, I drove home that night in Massachusetts, holding the Honda's bus-like steering wheel, through hills that Mailer too travelled, drove beneath silvery clouds and a heavy late-summer moon.

T.S. Eliot

William Kilbourn, Toronto

No one had noticed his presence there today during solemn eucharist at the Church of the Advent at the foot of Beacon Hill in Boston. The gloom of the high red-brick interior was made even more mysterious by the flickering candles, the red glow of the hanging votive lamps, the narrow shafts of spring sunlight and the clouds of incense drifting out from the sanctuary.

'If Shakespeare were here among us we would not recognize him,' the rector remarked to illustrate some point in his sermon. He spoke truer than he knew. For many of us in that church no living person was more revered than that ultimate man of letters, Thomas Stearns Eliot. But no one recognized him.

No one, that is, but the sleek worldly vicar who pulled me aside as I emerged into the bright sun. He pointed to the back of a lean jaunty angular gentleman propelling himself by cane towards the Back Bay subway station. 'Bill, why didn't you offer Mr. Eliot a lift back to Cambridge?'

I chased him down and asked him if he would come with me. 'How very kind,' said the great man, and he allowed himself to be steered back through the departing company of High Church devout, Episcopalian visitors, scruffy anglophile university students and Proper Bostonians from The Hill – the sort of people who would have thought it inappropriate to accost a person in the street as I had just done.

I introduced Mr. Eliot to my wife and two little girls and he then obediently folded himself into the back seat of my Austin and sat down beside the large, fully-coiffed, black-habited figure of Sister Felicia, a retired Smith College professor turned nun, who was holding our infant, Nicholas, on her lap. Sister Felicia was a little deaf and was aware only of a slightly epicene old man disturbing her brief weekly visits with her proxy godson. She held herself aloof from his gesture of greeting and his struggle to get enough purchase on the edge of the seat for the door to close.

I should have left well enough alone. As we drove off along the Charles River I told Sister Felicia, in a voice loud enough for even her to hear, exactly who it was that was sitting next to her. Her implacable silence was transformed instantly into a torrent of words and gestures worthy of St. Theresa in ecstasy. She went on and on about which of his poems her Smith girls had most adored and why.... I feared that I would never get a question in edgewise, or he a response. I had to content myself with the sight, through the rear-view mirror, of his intense eyes, the noble beak and the hint of a grin on his face. He was clearly amused. I longed for a pronouncement on the future of poetic drama, a comment on Dante, anything. But there was no way. The torrent of words from Sister Felicia continued relentlessly.

Eliot had just been reported somewhere or another as saying that the key to his new play, *The Confidential Clerk*, lay in Euripides' *Ion*. At a certain moment, when the baby made an unexpected twist or turn and Sister Felicia was momentarily distracted, I pounced in and commented that copies of *Ion* had since disappeared from all the university library shelves.

'Not in the original, I fear, Mr. Kilbourn,' he replied.

We stopped at an address off Brattle Street, and the aged eagle disengaged himself from his disciples and with a tip of his straw boater disappeared behind the lilacs.

Fidel Castro

Lionel Kearns, Vancouver

You can't play ball with the Commies, that's what they used to say when I was a kid growing up in the interior of British Columbia. But there I was, a few years later, squatting down behind the plate and squinting through the bars of a catcher's mask, the sweat running down into my eyes, as Fidel Castro fired the old *pelota* down on me from the pitcher's mound in the sports stadium of Santiago de Cuba. It was, as you might expect, a big moment.

But why me and Fidel? Well, the North American team was trailing the Cubans 16-1 in the bottom of the fourth, so we decided to switch pitchers to make the game less lopsided. Our pitcher went over to their team and Fidel began pitching for us. With the teams balanced in this way we were able to hold the Cubans down to a mere two additional runs during the rest of the game.

I had not worn catcher's equipment for years, and had not even thrown a ball for months. Nevertheless I held my mitt up there in the right place and managed to hang on to whatever Fidel threw at me. He had no fast ball at all, but his curve broke with an amazing hook, and his knuckleball came in deceptively slow. As I recall, he did not actually strike many out, but he gave up very few hits, with most of the batters grounding out or popping up flies. The Cubans, all of them university students except Fidel's brother Raul who was playing second base, had almost as much trouble hitting Fidel as we had earlier.

Near the end of the game Che Guevera put in an appearance. He stood there in his customary olive-green battle fatigues, smoked a cigar and watched. Being from Argentina, he was not such a committed baseball aficionado.

I had once seen a CBC television documentary on Cuba that featured Che extolling his theory and practice of voluntary labour. The camera had caught him standing amidst the high cane, machete in hand, commenting that socialism was the abolition of the exploitation of one person by another. That had made a lot of sense to me. I, too, was ready to swing a machete in the tropical sun to further such ideals. In fact, that was the reason I had applied to come on this student work visit to Cuba. I had not guessed that Che would be standing over by the dugout watching me play baseball with his pal Fidel.

There were thousands of foreign students in Cuba that year. The government had invited them to see first hand what the Revolution was all about.

After doing stints in the cane fields or other work projects, most of us had gathered in Santiago for the local carnival and the annual celebrations commemorating the initial strike of the revolutionary forces against the Batista regime. One morning Fidel showed up at the university where we were staying, gave us a little welcoming address, and challenged us to a game of baseball. So there we were.

The game took place on the afternoon of July 25, 1964, almost five years after Fidel, Che, Raul and the victorious guerrilla army from the Sierra Maestras had entered Havana, and a year after their revolution had survived the Bay of Pigs invasion by the American-backed contras. American warships were still blockading the island.

The night before the game I had been in the bleachers of this same stadium watching the Cuban National Ballet perform *Coppelia*. The day after the game I would listen to Fidel make an impassioned four-hour speech to a throng of over a million people standing and cheering in the 98-degree sun. At the end all of us would hold hands and sing The International.

Frenchy D'Amour

Fred Wah, South Slocan, British Columbia

I grew up in Trail, British Columbia, home of the Smoke Eaters. These world-famous ice hockey champions gave the people from Trail an inside track on fame. As did Frenchy D'Amour who was the second legendary person I met. (The first was Larry Kwan, the China Clipper, who played with the Smokies, later with Calgary and then down east somewhere.)

My dad was a very gregarious restaurateur who, with my granddad, ran the Elite (pronounced ee-light) Café downtown. As a Chinaman he had learned early to kowtow to the rich and powerful. He'd often sit the health inspector down to a free lunch in the kitchen of the café, or spike the mayor's coffee with rum at Christmas time. The local constabulary could frequently be found rifling down sugar doughnuts and coffee by the back door. My dad knew everyone who was anyone in this smelter town.

This particular Sunday afternoon in the spring of 1948 the whole town was buzzing about Frenchy D'Amour's triumphant return. There was even a parade down Cedar Avenue. But what most impressed me was that my father had invited Frenchy over to our house for a drink, and now here they were, sitting at the dining-room table, talking about the victory. I watched them drink. Or, rather, I watched Frenchy drink; my father had that Oriental disposition that prevented him from drinking very much. He'd pour, with a great deal of challenge and bravado, huge straight shots for his guests, yet rarely touch it himself. For a long time I thought he did it just to make asses of the high muk-a-muks. But when I saw him pouring drinks and chumming it up with Frenchy, I was really proud to see my dad joking around with the most famous person in Canada that day, in our house.

You have to understand that 1948 was the greatest year in the history of human civilization. Besides the huge floods along the Columbia and the Kootenay that spring, Frenchy D'Amour's rink lifted the Brier Tankard and brought the Dominion Curling Championship not only home to Trail but, for the first time in history, to British Columbia.

Bob Feller

George Bowering, Vancouver, British Columbia

You have to understand that 1948 was the greatest year in the history of human civilization, and that one of the most important things to happen in 1948 was that at last Bob Feller would get his chance to pitch in the World Series.

In 1948 if you were talking about singing you said Sinatra. If you were talking about hitting you probably said DiMaggio. But if the subject was pitching you started and ended all discussions with the phrase 'Bob Feller.'

Bob Feller did get his chance to start in a World Series game. In fact his Cleveland Indians beat the Boston Braves four games to two, and Feller started in the two games the Indians lost. Those losses, especially the loss in the opening game, formed the material of the sad heart sports story of 1948.

Feller should have won that first game. He pitched a two-hitter and lost 1-0 to Johnny Sain, the best pitcher in the National League. Moreover, the one run that crossed the plate had no business being there, and the proof was on hundreds of sports pages the following day and all the next winter. It is one of the most famous photographs in sports, Lou Boudreau laying the tag on the shoulder of Phil Masi, out by a foot and a half on Feller's great pickoff in the eighth inning. But National League umpire Bill Stewart called Masi safe, and he scored on the second Brave hit of the game.

There was a lot of noise in the open square of the old market in Victoria. There was also a sign in the window of the sports store in the corner of the market square. The sign said that Bob Feller would be there to sign autographs. This was forty years later.

Inside the sports store Mr. Feller was sitting at a card table around near the back. There weren't any customers around. Everyone was outside catching the free concert. But this was the kid who had come up to the majors at the age of seventeen and struck out seventy-six batters in the sixty-two innings he pitched that first year! Sitting at that card table he looked about the way he had looked during his first season, hair combed straight back with water, face that looked as if it had never left Van Meter, Iowa.

I walked right up and said 'hello,' or rather not 'hello' but some other word, as if there weren't any formality to get over. I am not good at talking to famous people. They scare the hell out of me. But then this great pitcher was up here in Victoria, Canada, and what would he think?

I put my hands about nine inches apart.

'Masi was out by this much,' I said.

'It was twice that,' he replied, quickly.

Tony Bennett
Eileen Chisholm, Hamilton, Ontario

I was working evenings at a small cigar and gift shop in the lobby of the Royal Connaught Hotel in Hamilton, Ontario. I looked up to attend to a customer and gasped at the striking resemblance to Tony Bennett, except that he was smaller in physical stature. I remarked that he resembled the singer and he smiled shyly from beneath his bushy eyebrows and said 'Perhaps because I *am* Tony Bennett.' I was astounded.

'I thought Tony Bennett was a much bigger person,' I said. He explained that movies or television added quite a lot to the size of a person. He spoke so quietly and gently that when he left I felt someone had tiptoed in and laid a gentle hand on my brow and with a shy gentle smile tiptoed back out, leaving me with a feeling of peace and happiness and without an autograph.

Elvis Presley

Chloe Lietzke, Oakland, California

I have been married twenty-three years, work in an office, am a mother, and keep active in Elvis Fan Clubs. Every year since 1981 I travel to Memphis and recapture the ecstasy of being with Elvis fans from all over the world. How did it start? Well, way back in August of 1956 I listened to all the Elvis records which had just been released by RCA and I liked them all. Elvis was so *different*, intense, spontaneous, wild, and the best performer I had heard on the radio at that time. Then, thanks to the Colonel I guess, Elvis came to my small home town of Orlando, Florida. It *was* small in those days: we had no large supermarkets or shopping centres. We lived a mile from downtown. I had not seen Elvis on television, because we had no television. And going to see a live concert was not something we normally did in those days, with my family or peers. I try to explain by saying I just wanted to go see A Famous Person, since I didn't have that chance with my former heart-throbs, Gregory Peck and James Dean, but I think it was more than that, some sort of magic, as evidenced by the following events.

There was no doubt about it: when I saw the ad I went right down to the drugstore and bought a ticket. Because we didn't have a lot of money I got a cheap one ($1.25). But three days before the show, I was getting more excited about seeing him, and, with uncharacteristic boldness (because the ticket admonished 'No Refunds,' and I was only fourteen) I went back and asked to exchange my ticket for a $1.75 one, for the possibility of sitting in the front row!

The day arrived. When I got there about fifty people were already on the doorsteps. I had talked my dad into driving me two hours early, at six. The doors opened at seven and the show started at eight. At about seven a man came out and said that $1.75 ticket-holders would be allowed in first. There was a considerably larger crowd by then, and past the ticket-taker it was mayhem! I was pushed and ran alternately down to the front. At the fifth row there was a seat near the middle. I screamed: 'Is that sate seaved??!' No one laughed at my tongue-twisting mistake or paid any attention to me at all so I made my way to it. There was such a feeling of excitement in the air that you wouldn't have left your seat for anything! We began chanting: 'We want Elvis!' People in the first rows were moving their chairs forward (they were folding chairs) and someone came on stage and announced that the show would not go on if the chairs were not moved back. They were moved back, but not as straight as they were originally.

Then there was the dull first part of the show. Scotty and Bill, a group of singers, unknown. There were some 'We want Elvis!' chants and again we were admonished. The doors were ajar to provide some cool air.

But suddenly it didn't matter; Elvis came out, in his green sportscoat, white shirt, white knit tie, black pants and white shoes, and it was mayhem again. Every girl screamed!

I was hypnotized. All I remember about the whole show that night is that he started out singing a song that had just been released by Gene Vincent, who sounded just like Elvis. 'Wellll, be-bop-a-lu-la – oops, wrong song!' Then he shifted to 'Heartbreak Hotel,' having to wait while the audience reacted to his joke. Someone had already told me that that was his standard opening joke in those days.

I have recently figured out that he must have been on about twenty minutes – about eight or nine songs. I cannot tell you what they were, besides 'Heartbreak Hotel,' and I'm pretty sure of 'Blue Suede Shoes' and 'Money Honey,' but I can tell you that I was totally unconscious of myself. You know that usually during a show you sit back, look around, notice other things. I was compelled to keep my eyes on Elvis every minute! Today, I can close my eyes and see clearly his smooth face. He was 'so cute,' as we said in those days.

On a deep level, I was completely 'there,' but on a conscious level, I was not there. It was a rare occurrence. On a physical level, when he moved like he did (much more freely and powerfully than on TV), it was incredibly thrilling. How could I resist? He was strong, masterful, yet also tender and lovable!

For days following I was still in a dream world, one like I have never experienced since. I wanted time to stand still, because each day I was farther from Elvis. I had very real fantasies of meeting him casually. No boy I knew measured up to him, yet at that time he was very real, like my boyfriends, not a star. I had *seen* him!!

I learned that a girlfriend had also been in the audience. She

Grey Owl

Ruthe Calverley, Richmond Hill, Ontario

The year was 1938. I was walking along Bloor Street and saw an apparition coming towards me: a tall, elegant North American Indian in full buckskin, bead and feathered regalia, accompanied by a sweet-faced female companion in matching attire.

I remained rooted to that central point of sidewalk watching wide-eyed as they approached, shimmering in the light, transforming the city around me. I hoped they would not disappear.

I gave a little bow of recognition and said: 'Will you come to tea with me, I am a painter and live right up there,' pointing to the third floor of an old mansion where Holt Renfrew was eventually built.

To my utter amazement they were delighted to accept my invitation, but added they could only stay for a short time, as they had another engagement.

I led the way up the stairs to my rooms, put the kettle on, grabbed an unprepared board, brush and tube of burnt umber, and began my lightning sketch of his regal profile.

A clock struck and I was suggesting a feather in his hair. They said they would be late. I asked him to sign his name with my brush at the bottom of the sketch. He printed: GREY OWL.

Through the years that sketch board has darkened to a rich copper tone, as authentically Indian as Grey Owl through his years.

His companion's name was Anahareo, which I think means Silver Dawn.

Norval Morrisseau

Gwendolyn MacEwen, Toronto

Out of Murray's Restaurant at Bloor Street and Avenue Road emerged a lanky figure in blue jeans splotched with a thousand different colours of oil paints. I did a double-take; then, thunderstruck, I approached him – avatar of Thunderbird himself, greatest of our native artists.

'Norval Morrisseau,' I said in an awed whisper. 'I am so happy to see you at last....'

'I am not Norval Morrisseau,' said Norval Morrisseau.

'Look,' I ventured, 'I'm one of your greatest admirers. I'm a writer, I've quoted you in some of my poetry.'

'All I want to know is where I can find a decent bacon and egg sandwich in this town,' said Norval, peering over my head.

'You mean a western sandwich?'

'I mean a decent bacon and egg sandwich. And where I can find it.'

'Have you tried the Varsity at Spadina and Bloor?' I asked.

'Oh,' he said, and turned to his companion – another tall, slim fellow who returned his look of exasperated boredom in the presence of this short, white female who was wasting their time.

'Do try the Varsity,' I pushed on, pointing west to Spadina.

'Okay,' said Norval, and swivelled around in the opposite direction and headed due east.

Leonard Cohen

Dianne M. Brady, Montreal

One night in the middle of winter I went to an art opening on St. Dominique Street in Montreal, and I saw this man. I went up to him and he said, 'This is my friend Bill and my name is Leonard. Would you like a beer ...?' I said sure. I then realized it was Leonard Cohen, and I told him that I liked his song, 'Like a Bird on the Water' ... and he corrected me by saying, 'Like a Bird on a Wire.'

I can't remember what else we said but he asked me if I wanted a smoked meat sandwich ... so I said yes ... and I felt as if my heart was racing a bit and I was somewhat infatuated with his eloquent (yet earthy) mannerisms.

So we went to the Main. As we were sitting there all these people came into the restaurant, and a couple of earnest student types came over to the table and said hello squeamishly and admiringly. I felt somewhat ignorant as I hadn't read *Beautiful Losers* or seen his video called 'Nightclubbing.' I felt a charismatic warmth of some sort, some kind of familiarity or déjà vu, like we'd met before or we were destined to meet again. I could hardly eat. He said he liked the Main 'cause it reminded him of Miami and at that time he was disillusioned with Greece (it was during all the trouble over there).

Next time we met it was at the Bar St. Laurent, another of his hang-outs. We did the same, that is we ate smoked meat. I had my video camera with me this time, and he'd arrived from playing a French police lieutenant in Miami that night. He was tired. It was about one o'clock in the morning. So we talked about the advantages of Miami as opposed to Paris, L.A., etc. Then we went to his house and I made another one of my art videos. I still have the video but I promised him I would never show it to anyone unless it was in an art context. I haven't shown it to more than twenty people and all settings were art-oriented. Anyone who has ever seen it says it is very good. It is more like a family photo album.

I keep in touch with Len but since I was away in an artist colony in Vermont last winter, and since I fell in love with someone, I've lost touch. I like him as a neighbour and he enjoys me likewise. I remind him of an artist friend in New York.

Dwight D. Eisenhower
David Hlynsky, Toronto

1960. I'm standing at attention with 55,000 other Boy Scouts along a rolling ribbon of new asphalt at the International Jamboree in Colorado Springs. We are waiting for Ike....

Suddenly this soundless black bullet of a Cadillac convertible swishes past, all round and soft as a Betty Boop cartoon, and Ike is standing up and waving at us like Elmer Fudd. We are trained to sleep in the mud, respect old ladies and murder reptiles with small explosives. We give Ike the official three-finger Scout salute.

I swear that there was no Secret Service and no driver ... just Our Leader, Ike, standing all alone, guiding his convertible by the gentle pressure of his spit-shined shoes.... General Fudd, the Old Bald Surfer. I know beyond question that some place in the great fossils of time this clean moment lies etched like a seamless Norman Rockwell painting....

In the ladies' washroom on the train home, we beat up a Congressman's son for stealing our Mexican snake-skin souvenirs. His confession was extracted under torture. I know now that he probably never touched the stuff.

Dizzy Gillespie
Don Druick, Montreal

It was a spring evening in Montreal in 1962 and I found myself talking with Dizzy Gillespie about time, about life, about music, and about the philosopher Henri Bergson. Gillespie was performing with his quartet at Le Jazz Hot, an upstairs jazz club in the Casa Loma on St. Catherine Street East. I was seventeen years old, studying philosophy at McGill University.

I was sitting by myself at a table by the bandstand, listening to what I have come to see as a great and classical repertoire, and I was enthralled.

During the break, Dizzy came off the stage, and began chatting up the audience from table to table as he wended his way to the bar.

I was reading Henri Bergson's *The Philosophy of Time*, and it caught his eye as he passed my table.

'Bergson,' he said. 'My my. My my my.'

He sat down.

'Now philosophy,' he said, 'now that's something that I *really* like. And time, well time especially, yeah, well, you know I *am* the boss, me and Henri.'

'Why is Bergson so complicated?' I said.

'It's not that complicated,' he said.

'What's it feel like to play jazz?'

'It's not that complicated either,' he said. 'It's not that time is anything more than who we are, you know.... You punch wind, you punch wind and blow, but don't look behind yourself 'cause then you are nowhere.'

Nothing was complicated to Dizzy that night.

'Oh, got to get back to work. Hey, it wouldn't do to be late. Well, the band really gives me shit if I'm the *last* one up on the stand. Yeah, it's been a blast. Hey, you're a good kid. Let me – well, anything in particular I can play for you?'

I thought, what what what what what. 'Play "Round Midnight."'

'"Round Midnight," ummmmm yeah.'

With a wink in my direction, it was the first number he played that set.

Victor Mature

P.K. Page, Victoria, British Columbia

World War II had just ended. I was holidaying in New York with a friend – both of us stage struck. We haunted Broadway – went to every matinee, every evening performance, and ate and drank wherever theatrical people were said to hang out. We hardly spoke to one another, so intent were we upon looking for the famous – none of whom crossed our paths!

Then towards the very end of our stay, who should we see in a late-night bar but Victor Mature? It was not he we were looking for – we had hoped for one of the greats.

'Go and pick him up,' my friend said. 'I dare you.'

There were few dares I wouldn't take in those days so I insinuated myself in beside him, ordered a drink and tried to engage him in conversation. Flattering conversation, fascinating conversation. Nothing I said or did earned me anything but the most withering of glances, and the amused grimaces of onlookers. Just what I would have done had he responded to my advances, I can't imagine, yet his rejection of them did nothing for my self-esteem.

Next morning I read in the paper that in the previous year Victor Mature had dated twenty small blondes. I, tall and brunette, felt better.

William Golding

Ken Mitchell, Regina, Saskatchewan

When William Golding made his cross-Canada tour a couple of years ago I was asked to entertain him when he touched down in Saskatchewan. I agreed without thinking – just the chance to engage in talk with the great man! 'What do you think he'd like to do?' I asked, and was told he'd expressed an interest in seeing a prairie farm. Dutifully, I lined up a range of possibilities – a few rusticated relatives and a Hutterite colony. When the moment arrived, though, the Goldings and their agent Charles thought they'd prefer a drive in the country, without leaving the car. Someone's feet were aching. Now what? Nobody but me thinks the countryside around Regina is scenic.

I set out for Moose Jaw, hoping something would appear, and what did was a sign advertising the Moose Jaw Wild Animal Park, a diverse collection of wildlife which includes a herd of bison. The park was closed for the season, but I swung the gate open and we drove in. The buffalo were nowhere in sight but as we approached the deer compound, a huge elk sprinted into view. I now remembered hearing about this bull on the radio – how dangerous he could be in rutting season. My guests began to rave about his massive rack of antlers, but all I could see – as he trotted towards the car – was the yard-long penis flopping under his belly.

Golding stepped out the back door of the car for a closer look just as the aroused elk charged the fence. 'Get back in!' I yelled. I couldn't tell if he was excited by Golding's flowing white beard or the blue station wagon, but with elk semen spraying in all directions, I couldn't take a chance on that flimsy wire fence that separated the old man from a ton of palpitating elk. Literary history would never tolerate a Nobel Prize winner being raped by an elk in Moose Jaw.

M.M.

Bill Berkson, Bolinas, California

Credit Tom Rogers with an assist. Once or twice a year, Tom, who was married to Ceil Chapman and managed her high-fashion dress design business, for which my mother did public relations, would invite me to share his season box on the third-base line at Yankee Stadium. On this particular day, however, there was no game, just an avuncular lunch with Tom and my eighth-grade classmate and fellow autograph hound Mason Hicks at Toots Shor's restaurant in the West Fifties, a meeting place for sports figures, writers, and assorted Hollywood and Broadway types. At the bar or hopping tables would be Max Baer, Gene Tunney, visiting ballplayers like Stan Musial, columnists Nick Kenney and Leonard Lyons, and perhaps a movie star or two like Dinah Shore with her husband George Montgomery. Mason and I had club sandwiches and Cokes with maraschino cherries and looked around while Tom made light with whomever came by the table. It was all vaguely glamorous but impeccable thanks to Tom's gentle, boozy, blushful Irish cheer.

Came the moment of parting, Mason and I found ourselves outside on this unusually quiet, summery, midtown side street. We turned to walk towards Fifth Avenue. About halfway up the block appeared a beige sackdress – this is circa 1953 – pumps and a flash of soft blonde permanent wave. There must have been other more identifiable features, but somehow we made a rapid computation of this mirage. Plain as day: Marilyn Monroe. And we sprinted straight for her, our ever-ready autograph books in hand.

We saw her turn into a building, slackened our stride and, taking deep preparatory breaths, followed through revolving doors. It was a narrow office building lobby, completely empty but for us and the woman standing waiting for the shiny brass door of the elevator to open. It was a time of wobbly knees and no second thoughts as Mason and I walked the length of the lobby, drew up and, with respectful mutters, extended one blank page each of the little padded leather albums for her to sign her name – 'Marilyn Monroe' – in ballpoint blue ink in a large, clear, barely slanting script. She smiled openly, as if appreciating the oddity of the situation from the angle of a couple of twelve-year-olds with whom a dream had so suddenly become complicitous. It was as if she enjoyed our company at that moment in a way neither of us was prepared to fathom. She made a little bounce, the elevator opened, and she withdrew from sight.

Tennessee Williams

John Lazarus, Vancouver

One evening in November 1980 I put on my best suit and went off to the theatre in a state of demented terror. The play was *Dreaming and Duelling,* which I had written with my ex-wife, and it was opening at Vancouver's Waterfront Theatre. It was my first full-length play that I thought had half a chance, and I was insane with anxiety. For my date, I had wisely invited a lovely, gentle woman who earned her living counselling assault victims at a crisis centre.

I sat engraving my fingerprints in Stephanie's arm as we watched the audience file in. There was Roger Hodgman, artistic director of the Vancouver Playhouse. And there with him was a ragged, elderly little figure in a car salesman's sports jacket and early Bob Dylan cap. It was Tennessee Williams, in Vancouver for a Playhouse production of *The Red Devil Battery Sign.*

I stared at the back of his head. He had recently walked out on a play by a Vancouver colleague, but maybe he'd stick around for this one: it was all about sex, death and handsome young teenage boys stripping to their underwear in the locker-room scenes. And indeed, when the house lights came up after the curtain call, he was still there.

I had not had a drink or a toke, and yet all evening I seethed with paranoia. I have since seen that the play is successful; but that evening I was simply unable to perceive the response, and afterwards, at the lobby reception, behaved as badly as I have ever behaved in my life. I believed in no one's praise. They were lying, it was a flop, they all hated it, nobody would tell me the truth. I was snarling at dear friends and well-wishing strangers. 'John! Congratulations!' 'What's *that* supposed to mean?'

Roger came up and said, perhaps in an effort to calm me, 'Would you like to meet Tennessee?' Aha! Here was one who might tell me the truth; one who had been there and back and had nothing to lose. Also, some day I could put it in a book.

Roger took me out to a small group milling about in front of the theatre. I heard a Southern accent say 'Is this him?' – and found myself locked in the firm bear hug of a rather small bear. I looked down into expensive tinted bifocals, ravaged skin, a tangled grey beard and a huge, vastly amused smile of yellow dentures. I inhaled bourbon.

'Ah enjoyed yoah play vereh much!' he said loudly.

'Thank you,' I mumbled.

'It had a beautiful rahs and fawl!' he shouted.

'Thank you,' I mumbled.

'It had a loveleh, pristine qualiteh!' he hollered.

'Thank you very much,' I mumbled.

I don't remember a great deal more. I introduced my ex-wife, of whom he seemed vaguely dismissive. A young man, author of the play Tennessee had walked out on, laughingly berated him. Tennessee invited me to lunch at the U.B.C. Faculty Club. I agreed. He told me to phone him at the Playhouse and we'd set the date.

For weeks I agonized over this simple, gracious invitation. Stories of his interminable, liquid lunches were already all over town. I didn't drink. Did I want to sit for hours listening to this strange, famous, garlanded old pagan telling me rambling anecdotes aged in bourbon, just to say I had done it? What if I brought the ex-wife and they hated each other, which seemed plausible? What if I didn't bring her and he made a pass at me, which ditto? What if the whole thing just turned into Lunch in Hell? I was unable to pick up the phone.

I saw him again at the opening of Red Devil, and decided, okay, this is it, let's do lunch. I went over, reintroduced myself, thanked him for his kind words to the press about my play, apologized for not calling, promised that this time we would do it, asked how long he was staying in town. 'I'm gwine home tomarrah,' he laughed. I apologized again. 'Well, if yeh didn't cawl, yeh didn't cawl,' he said with a shrug, and turned to the admirer on his left.

83

Phil Ochs

George Myers, Jr., Westerville, Ohio

I was attending the Royal University of Nairobi in 1973 and, on a green wooded hill a mile away, sharing a two-man room in the YMCA. One day a heavy-set man announced himself from the doorway, bougainvillea in bloom behind him on a makeshift trellis. He strode in, dragging an army surplus bag and a guitar, and dropped wearily on the cot facing me. He wore a funny blue cap, like a beret maybe, and fatigues. The army jacket was too warm for the weather. In my thinking about it I missed his name.

Pushed by indifference, the man reached into his duffel bag, withdrew a book or album and tossed it to me. It was *The Phil Ochs Songbook.* The man was Phil Ochs, folksinger and songwriter, author of any number of small hits from the sixties. He was disturbed I didn't recognize his name at the outset, but was pleased that I eventually did. I was twenty, not yet into my time. His time had passed, he said. Over the next three weeks he would say that the past was a terrible burden on him, that the 'movement' was dead, that there were no more issues, no more dragons to slay.

Ochs had just been mugged and beaten up by robbers in Tanzania and he was working his way through Kenya, sore throat, guitar and dungarees. Ochs said he was looking for a cause, to be 'reignited,' as he said it. He had set up a recording session at an EMI-affiliated studio in Nairobi and did produce, after much translation problems, a two-sider to be played on local jukeboxes, and it was after that he moved on.

My favourite memory of Ochs was when we attended *Once Upon a Time in the West* for the second time at a rundown old movie house in Nairobi. The Jason Robards-Henry Fonda film was his favourite, he said, and he knew its scenes forward and backward. The locals, however, did not. About two hours into the picture, the projectionist goofed up the order of the reels and played the finale too soon, and then continued with the out-of-order reel. I could understand a little Swahili by that time and could hear that no one in the audience seemed to notice, or care. The fact that one man could be shot and killed, then rise up again alive seemed perfectly okay to everyone.

Ochs was enraged, at first. He left his seat to talk to the projectionist and came back happy. I asked him what happened. 'You'll see,' he said. And I did see, for another three hours. He talked the projectionist into playing the reels in the right order. By lengthening the film to a marathon five-plus hours, we could watch Fonda live, be killed off, live again and then die a second time around. No one thought anything amiss, from what I could tell. Ochs was particularly pleased; he was laughing.

Andy Irvine & Hercules the Bear

Michael Elcock, Sooke, British Columbia

Andy Irvine had agreed to launch the fund raising for the European Paraplegic Games at a press conference at the Commonwealth Stadium in Edinburgh. It was quite a coup. Andy played rugby for Scotland. He was probably the greatest player the country had ever produced. He had scored more points than anyone in the international history of the game. I'd only seen him from the terracing along with 80,000 other fans, as he shimmied and deked his way through the English, or the Welsh.

The banquet room was full of press and assembled notables. The Lord Provost was there beside a retired brigadier with waxed moustachios, a pipe and leather elbow pads. Andy went round the room shaking hands. He was tall and open faced with a shy smile. Unassuming. As he came up to me a rumble and a bang rattled the picture window. We turned to look.

'What's that?' he asked. I was one of the organizers.

'It's Hercules the Bear. He's just finished a film shoot in the Hebrides and they've brought him down to give you a hand.'

Andy stared at me. 'It's all right,' I said quickly. 'He's quite harmless. It'll make a good picture for the papers.'

The door burst open and a huge brown bear crashed into the banquet room pulling his handler behind him at the end of a thick chain. Hercules lurched into a trestle table laden with sandwiches and tea. The table collapsed. Everyone squeezed back against the walls of the room. Hercules lumbered through the mess. A large dinner plate skittered across the floor and broke.

'Hairky!' shouted his handler. 'Behave yersell.' The bear swung him around at the end of the chain and set off across the room. The brigadier drew himself up and stood his ground bravely.

'Haud 'im Jimmie,' called a city official nervously.

'The prawns! The prawns!' yelled the handler. 'Gimme his bluidy prawns!' A young man rushed forward with a a large silver bowl in his hand. 'Pit it doon. There!' The handler pointed. Hercules lunged. 'Fer Christ's sake Hairky. Tak it easy.'

Hercules spun around with his nose up, sniffing. The handler swung round on the end of the chain and bounced off the broken table. He fell to one knee. The bear buried his snout in the silver bowl, making snuffling noises. The room began to relax.

Andy turned to me again. He seemed very calm. I could feel sweat under my arms. 'So what would you like us to do?' He indicated Hercules.

'Oh, just a handshake for the cameras. That sort of thing. I think that'll do it,' I said. 'And maybe if you could say something about the Games, and the quarter of a million pounds we need to raise to put them on.'

Andy nodded. The handler ambled up with the bear. The handler was soaked in sweat. Hercules had a glazed expression in his eyes. His bear-breath smelled overpoweringly of gin. 'Guid boy Hairky,' muttered the handler, ruffling the bear's furry neck. The press stepped forward, cameras ready. Andy held out both hands and took a huge paw.

'He's got no claws,' he whispered.

'Nae teeth either,' said the handler. 'He's quite harmless really.'

Neal Cassady

Diana Hartog, New Denver, British Columbia

Now, with people watching, it is always more difficult to do what you have to do. And people who have been drinking cheap red burgundy and doing acid and maybe a few bennies comprise a difficult audience – not because they are skeptics, but because they'll accept the undulation of walls, two dogs doing it missionary-style in the corner, and other stray miracles with aplomb; i.e., it is difficult to impress them with an act of skill – that it's real.

Neal Cassady was not one to rise to defeat.

The 'Dean Moriarty' of *On the Road*, Jack Kerouac's legendary novel, lies at this moment flat on his back under a wooden chair, ignoring the party.

True, to capture the attention of the jaded, one must keep talking, keep the balls in the air and in context – in this case the shabby upstairs rooms of a soon-to-be-razed Victorian in San Francisco, circa Buchannan and Post, 1966. The aroma of deep-fried zucchini wafts through the bullet-holes in the window from the Japanese restaurant next door and sinks to the floor: where Neal Cassady lies under the chair. He is gathering his strength for another attempt at a near-impossible feat. A continuous string of nouns, endearments, vectors, reversals, blasphemies and verbs issues from his throat as he talks to himself, pumps himself up – for though the body can hover indefinitely on the fuel from a single ecstatic act, the mind must eat. And Cassady's imagination, Rabelaisian, rotund from prolonged tonguing at the Alphabet but moving with that particular speed and grace of the obese, could turn knife-thin, mincing words. I heard him, I was there! – standing in the corner opposite the dogs. Imagine Yours Truly as a Third Eye, sober and of the size and naiveté of a Good Housekeeping Seal of Approval. I've moved closer, though in the glare from the overhead lightbulb it's hard to get a good look at Cassady's face, upturned in shadow. The chair straddling his chest is a plain wooden one, painted a chipped landlady green. It doesn't matter. What matters is that the chair listen as he delivers up an existential pep-talk to its rungs, or thereabouts. He's not crooning in the gentle persuasive tones of the Don Juan, not yet; instead his words jab with the speed and pyrotechnics of a self-taught liar, for he's trying to convince the chair to balance by a single hind leg on the tip of his index finger. But she won't. Bitch.

'Just this once just for me Babe come to *daddy* yeah' is a smooth approximation, somewhat like a dash, in his Morse Code as he squirms on his back for a better position under the chair. He cajoles its molecules now – for the benefit perhaps of a nuclear physicist and his well-dressed wife who sip discreetly at their drinks, witnessing what they must assume to be a monologue. But the chair is murmuring back! At least that's the impression, for Neal (I feel so much warmer towards him now) is pressing an ear to one of the chair's legs and nodding okay, okay.

To my left, the physicist is agreeing with his wife that it's possible, theoretically, to ascertain the centre of gravity of an object as complicated as a wooden chair – the point would float somewhere in the seat, towards the back. I imagine it as a tiny black dot, the size of the period that comes at the end of a normal sentence. Perhaps it is this period Neal is addressing, nudging it along faster with every word as he pleads with it to hold still. He grunts as again he lifts the chair above his chest – and oh! I am treated to a wide smile of flesh as his sweatshirt rides up on his stomach.

With the chair aloft, he then tilts the weight to the finger of one hand. He must now locate that tiny black dot in the dark and align it directly above his fingertip. Okay baby okay okay okay. He's now ready to withdraw all support and simply balance the precariously tilted chair on his index fingerprint ... steady ... steady....

It crashes to the floor.

After another hour or so, I wander off to find, among the guests, my future husband.

Yevgeny Yevtushenko

Stephen Scobie, Victoria, British Columbia

In the summer of 1982, while the nations of the world were engaged in conflict on the soccer fields of the Word Cup tournament, I was attending a poetry festival in Köln, West Germany. It was one of those idealistic affairs dedicated to literature as an instrument of peace and international understanding, and the delegation from the Soviet Union was headed by Yevgeny Yevtushenko. He came accompanied by two other alleged writers or professors, who were widely taken to be KGB watchdogs.

I met up with Yevtushenko one evening, in the middle of an immense cocktail party at a radio station; we were both looking for a TV, and the one place we couldn't find a TV was in a radio station. We had been briefly introduced before, and he knew that I was Scottish by birth – the point being that Russia and Scotland were about to play each other in the World Cup, and we both desperately wanted to see the game. So together we abandoned the conference, the dignitaries, and the cocktail party, and set off for a hotel bar.

The situation was this: it was the last match of the qualifying round. Russia had already advanced to the next round, so the result was not vital for them; but Scotland had to get a win to go on. At first it seemed as if they might; they were playing much better than the Soviets, running rings around them in fact, but without scoring. Yevtushenko was getting more and more angry. 'Run!' he was yelling at the screen (in English, for my benefit). 'Fools! Cripples! Even Brezhnev could move faster than you do!'

We had ordered wine and hors d'oeuvres in plentiful quantities. Yevtushenko began telling me how he had used to play soccer for a team in Moscow. 'I was a goalkeeper,' he said, 'and I was very good, I never dropped a ball. They used to call me Sticky Gloves.'

Then suddenly, quite against the run of play, the Russians scored a goal – a scrambled, fluky kind of affair, but a goal nonetheless. Yevtushenko leapt to his feet (he is very tall), raised his arms in triumph above his head, and shouted: 'GOAL!!' Then abruptly he stopped, and bowed to me, formally, from the waist. 'I apologize,' he said, 'on behalf of my country.'

Scotland did score later, and the game ended in a draw, which was not enough. We had drunk a lot of wine; we had not discussed poetry. In a final gesture of contrition, Sticky Gloves paid the bill, then vanished into the German night, in search of another party.

Yevgeny Yevtushenko
Rita Dove, Durham, North Carolina

As a young, aspiring poet eager to assemble reports on 'real' writers and how they lived, I had heard a ménage of anecdotes about the exuberant Yevtushenko. His prodigious consumption of liquor and women fulfilled the prevalent requirements for a Modern Romantic Poet (who was always male, naturally); and according to legend, the thrill of the chase was as desirable as the feast afterwards. So I was prepared for a full-court press when introduced to him years later at a writers' conference in Cologne, West Germany. And he used his height to full advantage, manoeuvring me into a corner, his cocktail held aloft on a level with the pale blue eyes slanting above high-pitched tartar cheekbones, as a modulated voice poured its British-tinted blandishments over me: 'At last I meet the American poet! But so young – and so lovely!'

I nodded, backing up, and slipped away when an awestruck author from Mali pressed him for an autograph. I was a novice at what I know now to be male conference behaviour; and as the sole representative from the United States with only one book of poetry under my belt, I felt more than a bit insubstantial. Besides, I was three months pregnant and feeling wobbly, not to mention non-confrontational. The conference, subtitled 'Writers for Peace,' went on for a week and was as long-winded and pussy-footed as every conference I've been to since, although this one had more than its share of chain-smokers. Since I knew the location of every bathroom in the building, I managed to elude Yevtushenko whenever I spied his towering approach through the crowds ... until the last evening, when I thought I was home-free.

On that evening, the conference commemorated itself with a marathon reading, followed by a sumptuous reception, at a museum in a nearby industrial town. Yevtushenko was the anchorman; he bounded up on stage, the image of vital, male, entrepreneur spirit, nothing up his sleeve or in his hands (his poetry recitations are famous for their near-operatic drama) ... and announced that he was dedicating his reading to 'my beautiful American colleague, Rita Dove.' And afterwards, bearing down on me (I thought

I was safe, since I was standing with my husband), he turned on boyish-smile-number-three.

'Well, did I succeed?' he demanded.

'Succeed in what?' I asked, taking a step backwards.

'In seducing you with my words.'

How does one respond to such a frontal attack? Trapped between my feminist belligerence (should I sock him in the gut, or wheel on an imperious heel and march away?) and the bewildering fact that my husband stood by grinning (Why didn't *he* sock him? Does his unconcern mean I'm over-reacting? Could this be *innocent*? Wait a minute – I'm the feminist here! And what if I walked away and my husband didn't follow?), I merely gaped.

'Come, tell me,' Yevtushenko cooed. 'How far did I get? Did I at least reach your knees?'

I cast a despairing glance at my husband, who had blithely turned away to chat with Gabor, a Hungarian playwright we had befriended. I overheard Gabor mutter, 'Just a minute.' He winked, strode over to the buffet table and pulled a long-stemmed rose from the centrepiece. He was back to our frozen triangle before the butler could release an outraged gasp. With just a little more old-world charm than reasonable he bowed, extending the rose with a flourish.

'Rita,' he said, 'this rose is from Andrey Voznesensky.'

Yevtushenko wheeled on his heel and marched off at a dignified-but-less-than-imperious pace. And I've loved Voznesensky's poems ever since.

King George VI

Jim West, Jr., Prince Rupert, British Columbia

My late father, Police Constable Jim West of Stratford-upon-Avon, Warwickshire, was a driver at divisional police headquarters during World War II.

The day following the air raid on Coventry, the late King George VI visited the devastation. Constable West was ordered to rendezvous with a black limousine at the Oxfordshire border and escort the vehicle to Coventry.

Security was tight, no one knew who was in the limo until on a lonely stretch of the Banbury to Warwick road the limo stopped suddenly. Out stepped King George VI who looked at my dad and said, 'It is quite all right, officer. I'm just going to urinate behind the hedgerow.' My father stood there at attention while His Majesty had a pee.

Dad later showed me on numerous occasions the exact spot where this little incident took place.

Dollar Brand

Penn(y) Kemp, Flesherton, Ontario

I had been helping organize a Dollar Brand concert as part of a jazz series at 'A Space,' the alternative gallery in Toronto. We'd put someone on the door, someone to manage seating. But I preferred to stay back, out of sight, behind the performer. Dollar had just finished a virtuoso spin when he appeared. The piano was still resonating out front. What I didn't realize was that our ordinary back room at 'A Space,' where all the paperwork was done, was now Dollar Brand's dressing room. Sweating a hurricane of energy after the last chord, he burst backstage at intermission. I was in his way, standing at the table. I turned around and was enveloped. We ricocheted apart and I, carefully conditioned, muttered, 'Oh excuse me, I'm glad to meet you,' and backed out. He blew me a kiss and sank into the swivel chair I'd been in. For the second part of the performance, I crept back into that chair and listened, not moving.

Hannelore Schmatz
Christopher Ondaatje, Toronto

Although I had met Arne Naess before, my most momentous meeting with him was at the end of May 1985 very soon after he had led the successful Norwegian expedition to the top of Mount Everest. He had lost an incredible amount of weight, and although he was very pleased with the climb he clearly had taken an enormous emotional and physical battering. We flew back to London together and he told me many hair-raising stories. Best of all was a hitherto well-kept secret among Everest climbers.

All climbers are warned that one potentially fatal thing is to sit down for a rest while in an exhausted state. Once you do, it is almost impossible to get up, and the horror of this warning is brought to full realization when you climb the narrow trail before the final ascent to the summit. This is because in order to get to the top of the world's highest mountain, exhausted climbers have to make their way around and past the seated, frozen body of the young German climber Hannelore Schmatz who has been sitting on the icy path since the autumn of 1979. Her blonde hair still blows in the breeze; her knapsack is still slung over her shoulder, and the calm, tight-lipped expression on her face remains to remind climbers of the dangers of taking a rest.

Willie Mays

Paul Auster, Brooklyn, New York

My devotion to baseball began during the 1954 World Series. I was seven years old and the New York Giants became my team. After their sweep of the heavily favoured Cleveland Indians, it was only natural that I should have fallen in love with the men in the black-and-orange hats. Of all the players on that team, Willie Mays was the one I followed most passionately.

In the spring of 1955 I was invited to my first major-league game. Friends of my parents had box seats at the Polo Grounds, and six or seven of us went along to watch the Giants play the Milwaukee Braves. It was a warm May night, and if I don't remember much about the game, I do remember the overwhelming impression it made on me: the noise of the crowd, the flood lights shining on the green grass, the utter whiteness of the bases.

After the game my parents and their friends sat talking in their seats until the stadium had emptied out. In order to leave, we had to walk across the diamond to the centre-field exit. In all other ball parks, the locker rooms are behind the dugouts, but in the Polo Grounds (an ancient structure that has since been torn down), the lockers were located in a little house that jutted out from the centre-field wall. To my amazement, just as we approached the wall, I saw Willie Mays standing there in his street clothes. Trembling with awe, I approached my hero and forced some words out of my mouth, 'Mr. Mays,' I said, 'could I please have your autograph?'

'Sure, kid, sure,' he said. 'You got a pencil?'

As it turned out, I didn't have a pencil. Nor did my parents. Nor did any of their friends. Willie Mays stood there watching me in silence as I asked one adult after another the same question, and when it became clear that no one in the group had anything to write with, he turned to me and shrugged. 'Sorry, kid,' he said. 'Ain't got no pencil, can't give no autograph.' And then he walked out of the stadium into the night.

I remember the tears that fell down my cheeks and how embarrassed I felt to be crying, but there was nothing I could do to stop myself.

Since that day, I have always carried a pencil with me. As I like to tell my son, that's why I became a writer.

Pat Nixon

David A. Smith, Fairfield, Connecticut

In the fall of 1956, Vice-President and Mrs. Richard Nixon paid an unexpected campaign visit to Glendale, California. Their route passed Glendale High School where I was a junior. Classes were dismissed for the appearance.

Leaving class to see a mere politician, even if he was Vice-President, seemed strange. Anyway, cars not politics were my passion.

The Nixons were in a brand-new Lincoln Continental. It was one of the first of the elegant Continental convertibles of the period, similar to the car in which John Kennedy later died, and the first one I ever saw. Those Continentals were the first four-door convertibles manufactured in the U.S. in almost twenty years. I had pored for years over pictures of four-door Phaetons of the twenties and thirties with a sense of loss.

I was stunned by the car's quiet grace, its sleek simplicity as it stood on Broadway in front of the majestic old Spanish colonial school. It was an esthetic thunderbolt in contrast to the fins growing annually larger and larger on almost every other car. My best friend, Carl, and I rushed forward uncharacteristically into the throng pressing against the Lincoln.

To address us, the Vice-President stood on the leather back seat, his wife sitting beside him in an orderly sea of 2,500 carefully dressed students, reminiscent of those she had known as a teacher herself. Mr. Nixon launched into what the high-school annual carefully recalled as an 'extemporaneous' speech.

'Carl,' I said, awestruck by the car and in a voice as loud as Nixon's, 'just look at those hubcaps! Wow! Are they beautiful.'

Mrs. Nixon, her face powdered and strained, leaned menacingly out of the car towards me.

'You,' she hissed. 'Be quiet. You'll never have a chance like this again in your life.'

I shrank dumbly back and Carl moved sheepishly away from me.

Senator Eugene McCarthy

William Corbett, Boston

He rounded the corner of a friend's house in Vermont. It was 1974. I was thirty-one and as eager to impress as I was to be impressed. McCarthy didn't stint me. We talked of baseball, boxing and Yeats' late revisions. He told stories about the Kennedys and described a lunch with Henry Kissinger. Had I never met him again I could have vouched for his charm, intelligence and gift for flattery. But I did meet him again for dinner twice at the same house. He spoke both times of the Kennedys, each time a little more bitterly of Bobby Kennedy, and he told again of his lunch with Kissinger. McCarthy was cordial and remembered me as a poet and so told for the second and third times of a poem about Nixon he had read in which Nixon's voice comes from the radio as honey, rivers and waves of honey.

Both times I left McCarthy I admired him less. It was not because he came across as exceedingly bitter. At our first meeting this was something I convinced myself we could share. I too was bitter at Kennedy, Kissinger and Nixon. That we were bitter for different reasons went right by me. What disturbed me was that McCarthy had repeated himself in such a way that it was clear he no longer heard what he was saying, could no longer imagine the effect his stories might have on his listeners. I assume he told these stories at many similar evenings to many other people who could offer nothing of their own in return. He remained charming and polished as only politicians (I have now met two or three) can be, but he was making hollow noises. As I judged him harshly I began to see how hollow I had been, how quick to put on airs, most readily the air of attention, from the moment we met. Now, ten year after our last dinner, it seems like a three-act play in which I played a role I am somewhat ashamed to know I had in me.

Glenn Gould

Bernice Eisenstein, Toronto

I was a teller in a large downtown Toronto bank in 1976, and I felt displaced, uncomfortable and transient. The job was a temporary means to an end, not a career decision. And with that position I remained aloof, efficient and worked on automatic pilot until 3:30 p.m. every day.

One day a very tall, solidly built man came into the bank.

'Steve Garvey!' everybody said.

'Who?' said I.

The tellers went into a huddle, then blushed and dashed for the phones to call their husbands to tell them Steve Garvey had just come into the bank. I went back to work, aware that some vital piece of cultural information was beyond my grasp. I had no idea who Steve Garvey was. My knowledge of sports greats ended with Frank Mahovlich. As a child my father allowed me to stay up late so I could enjoy his excited Yiddish expletives during the Stanley Cup playoffs.

Another day, another dollar. The one advantage to the design of most banks is the feeling of being encased in glass. For me, that prompted a lot of daydreaming. But then, perhaps counting money puts most people into a daze. Just like elevator music, or being put on hold on the phone.

The first thing I saw were these beautiful, too-thin, waxen, long fingers handing me a cheque for deposit. It was a CBC royalty cheque made out to Glenn Gould. I looked up and saw a dark hat and oversized winter coat enshrouding quiet delicacy. The transaction was quickly completed and Glenn Gould turned around, left the bank and entered his waiting limousine. All on a warm spring day. No heads turned.

'Glenn Gould!' I said

'Who?' said everybody.

I quit the bank the next day.

Glenn Gould

Felix Tyndel, Toronto, Ontario

We were in high school when we 'met' Glenn Gould. He was a customer on Loftus' paper route and we got reports of their brief threshold encounters: how, for instance, Gould would jump back from the door, unshaven and dishevelled, with a brisk 'Yessir.' There followed some rummaging, a large bill and retreat *sans* change. Did Paul and I want to see the hermitage on St. Clair Avenue? No debt was outstanding but we might dare to knock just the same.

The old brick building is shamelessly unprepossessing. Finding the side entrance open, we climbed up and waited in the stairwell so our huffing would not draw attention. Then the three of us broached the hallway.

A dim, carpet-muffled corridor. From behind the end-door, atonal piano music. And suspended in the air right around us, a spirit's voice unreeling an amelodic tune. Two threads, clearly unconnected, parallel, never-to-meet. Surely a philistine's TV confronting the maestro's keyboard. Check that. First door. Second door. Sounds fading. Steps retraced; crescendo. This, then, was it. The famous ghostly singing, unfettered by listener or microphone, glorifying the playing it so curiously accompanied.

We dared not knock; we stood listening. A floorboard creaked and we high-tailed it out.

Carson McCullers
William Corbett, Boston

It was 1964, and I was twenty-one and in my senior year at college when I went with a friend to interview Carson McCullers. She lived in Nyack, New York. We rang her doorbell and a large black maid in a black uniform answered. When we gave our name she shut the door in our faces to open it a moment later. She invited us into a living room where McCullers sat in a corner chair, her left side towards us, wearing a robe. She did not rise to greet us. She couldn't as several strokes had left her bedridden as well as having paralyzed the right side of her face. She drank from a tall silver stirrup cup. When, three hours later, we left and I crossed the room to shake her outstretched hand I smelled the bourbon she had sipped throughout the interview. She forgot to offer us a drink and when she did it was Coca-Cola which was welcome as we were parched by the intensity of listening to her but not so welcome as a stiff drink would have been.

McCullers spoke haltingly one ... word ... at ... a ... time ... and ... then a cluster ... followed ... by.... I soon started sweating through my shirt. She said she could no longer read but had *Dubliners* read to her every year. Recently, when she was being wheeled from her house to an ambulance, she looked up to see a sky as blue as the sky Prince Andrei saw in *War and Peace,* and she was ready to die. *The Heart is a Lonely Hunter* came about when she understood that of the three men walking around in her head two couldn't talk. This is what I remember and her frail body, bony arms and legs thin as a sparrow's. As we were being shown out a second maid came in to carry this tiny bundle upstairs to her bed.

Ernest Hemingway
Terence Keough

Bilbao was a long way from Jaca over narrow mountain roads. But Pierre said a bullfight featuring the rivalry of Luis Miguel Dominguín and Antonio Ordóñez was not to be missed.... In Bilbao we bought our tickets for the *corrida*, the medium-priced *sol y sombra*, sun for the first hour, shade later. In the presidential box at the *plaza de toros* was the wife of the head of state, Doña Carmen Polo de Franco. Everyone who mattered was at this *corrida*. It was an important fight.

It was on his second bull that Dominguín was gored. The big black bull caught him against the horse of the picador, piercing his thigh with his horn and pushing him against the horse. The crowd gasped. Ordóñez – and Jaime Ostos, the other *torero* on the card – leaped into the ring with their capes and led the bull away. Dominguín was quickly hand-carried out of the ring. Then Ordóñez fought Dominguín's bull and killed him.

When the fight was over and people were leaving the plaza, we spotted Hemingway in the expensive seats below us, standing with a too-thin, wan-looking girl of seventeen or so. He wore a brown-and-white-checked pancake cap and a pair of sunglasses with disconcerting yellow lenses. His head angled slightly forward from his body, as if he were compensating for the sore back that was the legacy of his two African plane crashes.

We hopped over the iron barriers and groped our way through the crowd to where he was standing and obviously soaking in the atmosphere of the end of the *corrida*. We asked him to autograph our tickets. In a surprising mid-western accent, he asked us where we were from. He had been where each of us was from.

But I wanted to know about Dominguín. 'How is Dominguín?' I asked.

'He'll be okay,' he said. 'It isn't serious.'

But in *The Dangerous Summer*, it is clear that the only word he had at this point was that the horn 'had gone up into the abdomen but they did not know yet if there was any perforation.' It was not until later that they knew for sure Dominguín would be all right. The horn had pierced the same route as an earlier wound in

103

Málaga. But Dominguín would never fight again. The rivalry had been decided.

We chatted about skiing in Austria, though I don't remember why, and then Hemingway left for the Carlton Hotel, where he was staying. The last I saw of him was his broad back as he left the plaza, his hand resting like a grandfather's on the shoulder of the wan young girl.

Ernest Hemingway

Martin S. Chase, Kentfield, California

My best friend Peter and I were able to cajole our parents into a trip to Havana for the spring semester break in 1950. Pre-Castro Havana was one of the glittering jewels of the Caribbean and the centrepiece of the city was the Hotel Internacionale.

In old-town Havana was a world-famous bar called either El Floradita or La Florida, depending on your preference. It had a dark mahogany bar about four furlongs in length and was manned by five very stuffy-looking bartenders. It was a meeting place for both the celebrities and the lowly. La Florida was well known for a concoction of its own called the 'Papa.' It was a basic daiquiri (lime juice, rum and sugar), except that the citrus was fresh grapefruit and the sugar was omitted. It was served in a monstrous chalice-like vessel that was at least three times the size of a normal drink. I hardly need add that it was lethal. The establishment seated two hundred at small cabaret tables. One side was open to the street and the square beyond. They served dinner in the rear.

The name Papa, of course, referred to Ernest Hemingway, and he was widely known and greatly admired throughout Cuba under that sobriquet. It was during this time that Hemingway was writing a trilogy about fishing and the sea, yet to be published in its entirety, although *The Old Man and the Sea* was one part.

My friend and I were not at La Florida by accident but by careful design. We knew this was Hemingway's favourite haunt, that he lived only a few miles from town, and that he had a rather severe need to keep his whistle wet. Peter was a collector of Hemingway's first editions and both of us had read most everything he had written, so the opportunity of meeting him was almost irresistible. As shadows lengthened and the cocktail hour approached, we would go down to La Florida in hope of catching sight of the great man. Three nights of 'Papas' were becoming ruinous to our health, but on the third evening our patience was rewarded. In strode Papa, waving to several friends and greeting the staff and owner. He was white-haired, barrel-chested, sunburned and hearty. With Mary and a dapper little man from Vienna he stood at his accustomed place at the end of the long bar and reached for the Papa that had already been poured.

Then it started. The tourists began passing him notes, autographs, invitations to join their tables, telephone numbers. The bartenders were the messenger boys for this blizzard of papers. Interestingly, Hemingway read most of the notes he received but he refused them all. It was obvious that we would have no chance unless we radically changed our method of approach. We set to work to devise a message that would almost demand a response.

Across the River and through the Trees had recently been published. It was clearly not vintage Hemingway and was widely panned by the literati, a few of whom thought the old man had had it. Papa was particularly testy because the main character, the Major, was the author himself in thin disguise. Just before we left for Cuba, E. B. White, *The New Yorker's* chief spear thrower, wrote an hilarious satire entitled 'Across the Street and into the Grill' in the staccato Hemingway style. Our note to Papa inferred that the satire was far superior to the novel, and discriminating readers should buy *The New Yorker* rather than the book and save themselves fifteen bucks.

Bingo! A barracuda hit our line. Papa turned bright red and bellowed. He demanded to know who wrote this slander. The bartender pointed an accusing finger at us, and we were summoned 'into court' prior to being executed. He raged and ranted at us, the Cuban government, the critics, the Internal Revenue Service, sycophants, cowards and bastards throughout the world. After a few more Papas he ripped open his shirt and told Peter to take his best shot. Peter broke his hand on Hemingway's solar plexus. Then it was Peter's turn to take Papa's best shot. One punch right in the middle of his chest spun him backwards across the room into a pile of stacked chairs. Fortunately he survived.

We were at La Florida for about seven hours. Somewhere along the way we had huge steak sandwiches chased down by other Papas. And the most poetic thing I heard Hemingway say all evening was his description of urinating on the autumn leaves in Ketchum, Idaho.

Quentin Crisp

Ian Young, Toronto

During the late seventies I lived in New York City, in an apartment just off Lafayette Street.

Early one afternoon I was walking home down Third Avenue at around 11th Street. Walking a few yards in front of me was a dapper man wearing a broad-brimmed hat whom I recognized as Quentin Crisp. This was shortly after Mr. Crisp, Larry Kramer and Andrew Holleran had been denounced as 'enemies' by the Gay Activist Alliance, presumably for writing the truth instead of the required politically correct line. Though my sympathies were with these fellow writers, I had never met any of them.

As Quentin Crisp and I each made our way down the avenue, a young man on the other side of the street caught sight of Mr. Crisp, dashed across the road, grabbed the broad-brimmed hat, threw it on the sidewalk and marched off.

In the few moments this took, I had caught up to the surprised Mr. Crisp. I picked up the hat, dusted it off quickly and handed it to him. He thanked me graciously, and we continued our separate journeys.

Michael Cardew

Carole Itter, Vancouver, British Columbia

A blind date when I was about nineteen is the connecting pivot to a brief meeting with a very special person. Nothing whatsoever came of the blind date; we both carried remnants of full-blown acne and were so extremely shy that we found out virtually nothing about the other. Some fifteen years later, I was sitting on the deck of a large ferry crossing an inlet on British Columbia's coastline with my two-year-old on my knee. Near me sat a man slightly greying at the temples, with a beard trimmed to mark him of the academia and a toddler mounted on his shoulders. He said hello and recalled the blind date; I recalled neither his face, his name nor the occasion until he spoke further. In the passing years, we'd acquired enough social graces to overcome our shyness and ask at least a few questions. After taking his B.A., he'd spent a few years 'bumming around' Africa but then returned to university and was now teaching in the department of chemistry.

Since I knew nothing about chemistry, I asked him what he did in Africa. He spent those years forgetting academics and tried to become a potter, working with the English-born grandfather of pottery who was living there at the time. And I *had* heard of this great man, Michael Cardew, because I'd hung around potters over the years and of course I'd read his excellent books, such as *Pioneer Potter, Nigerian Pottery* and *The Chronicle of Abuja*. So finally there was some topic in common.

On this ferry ride, he was going to visit his elderly parents who lived in the coastal town of Gibson's and he added that his parents were storing his immense collection of Michael Cardew's pottery from his African period at their home. I was going farther up the coast to a large piece of forest and clearing that I shared with other painters, potters, filmmakers, poets.

Not too many summers passed, and as usual I was squatting at my little outdoor firepit near the small shack preparing a meal for some close friends, all mothers with young children. We were a motley-looking bunch, sunburnt, half-clothed, quite dirty and sweaty; our young children naked and covered with mosquito bites as well as dirt. We had heard that the great English potter, the now-elderly Michael Cardew, was making a brief visit to the land that day as part of a cross-Canada tour. Specifically he was visiting Mick Henry whose pottery was on another part of the property. We thought it prudent to stay well out of the way with our gaggle of small noisy children. Which was exactly what we were doing, huddled around the firepit, when we heard the large retinue of Cardew and friends approaching on a little-used trail through the rainforest. I knew that their only means of getting farther was to pass right through my outdoor 'dining room,' a couple of cedar slabs set up near the firepit. Mr. Cardew was instantly recognizable, a wiry narrow mountain of a person with a huge shock of silver-white hair and eyes that sparkled on a wrinkled face, and he charged out of the dense forest and smack into our campsite with all the enthusiasm of Dr. Livingston.

It was a little embarrassing for both groups as neither had expected to meet the other and there were too many people to begin introductions. None of us was wearing enough clothes to actually receive such esteemed visitors. My shack was eight feet wide and twelve feet long so I certainly couldn't invite everyone in for tea. The youngest child had been sitting on a plastic potty near the outdoor 'dining room' and was yelling for his bottom to be wiped. Something had to be said other than 'pleased to meet you, sir, I've read your books,' so I overcame my shyness with a gulp and as succinctly as possible mentioned the large collection of his pottery from Africa which was now just seven miles down the coast, omitting that my only connection to it was through a blind date eighteen years ago.

Well, his reaction was phenomenal. He became so excited as he recalled the young Canadians who worked with him in Africa and he talked a full ten minutes in rapture before his large retinue moved awkwardly out of our campsite. Dinner got served, bottoms got wiped and we all remarked that, yes indeed, that was a very great man.

The finest part came much later when I heard that Michael Cardew frequently related the same story after his cross-country tour – how he'd been walking through a narrow trail on the coast of British Columbia, brushing past enormous ferns and huge cedars, when he came upon a small group of women by a firepit who told him that a large collection of his African pottery was stored just down the road and he marvelled again and again at what a small world we live in.

Cesar Romero

Ken Norris, Montreal

In 1980 I was in Los Angeles visiting my friend Gary who worked at 20th Century Fox. He was living with a girl named Sandy who had left her husband so that she could become the next Lucille Ball. One afternoon Sandy came home and told us that a casting director she knew had invited us to Cesar Romero's sixty-fifth birthday party. When she told us that the party was at Lynn Carter's house Gary and I got excited; we thought she'd said Lynda Carter, who at that time was playing Wonder Woman on television.

We were a bit disappointed when we got to the party and were greeted by a hostess who wasn't Wonder Woman. I might mention that in 1980 I had very long hair and a bushy beard; I looked a bit like a Quebec lumberjack. My hairiness seemed to distress the party hostess somewhat. I was wearing a corduroy jacket borrowed from Gary. The people at the party were quite formally dressed. Cesar Romero was wearing a suit and tie.

It proved to be a pretty dull party, and no one incredibly famous was there. Gary and I wound up standing in a corner close to the bar with Jesse, the guy who plays the Maytag repairman. He told us some pretty entertaining off-colour jokes. Sandy was off somewhere talking to the casting director. I was guzzling Perrier.

It was a cocktail-hour affair, and after a couple of hours it started to wind down. As people got ready to leave they went to shake hands with Mr. Romero and wish him a happy birthday. So we did too. When I approached him, Mr. Romero looked a bit dubious about shaking hands with a hippie – and I thought I saw a tightening in his jaw – but he accepted my best wishes graciously.

I wouldn't have washed my hand if I'd realized how important this event would prove to be to my mother when I told her about it sometime later. 'Cesar Romero,' she said in what was almost a heaven-struck sigh, her eyes glazing over as she pictured the romantic Latin lover of the fifties films. 'Cesar Romero!'

Yoko Ono

Ken Norris, Montreal

I once sold a copy of Carlos Casteneda's *The Teachings of Don Juan* to Yoko Ono. It was 1974. I was playing in a rock band called Bogart and working at the New Yorker Bookstore at the corner of Broadway and 89th Street.

On a slow Sunday morning I was reading the *New York Times* when two women came in. One was Yoko Ono. She was wearing a terrific-looking fur coat (I guess it was winter). She asked me for a copy of *The Teachings of Don Juan* which I dug out of the back of the store. I remember feeling somewhat disillusioned at the time; if she and John knew everything (which I assumed they did), why hadn't she read the book before? Even I'd read it, back in 1969 while visiting San Francisco.

I also remember wanting to ask Yoko how John was, but they were separated at the time (he was in L.A. with May Pang) and I thought the question might upset her. So I just sold her the book.

Anon.

Peter McGehee, Toronto

Saw your picture in *Newsweek*. The 'Face of Aids' issue. In the twelve pages of headshots. Selections from the death toll, month by month.

Your obit said you were in the Peace Corps, that you worked as a lawyer and with poor kids in the inner city. I never knew that. It didn't mention your Bisexual Marriage book. It didn't mention the Donahue show or the lecture circuit or the video you made for PBS. I remember that video – the clips of your wedding, the clips of your son whom no one talks about, who has something wrong with him.

You came to our university as part of our speaker series. I was on the committee and picked you up at the airport. We'd already had Burroughs, Isherwood, and Armistead Maupin, so I was used to people like you. I was ready.

You were into fisting. I'd read that somewhere – *The Gay Sunshine Interviews*, the *Advocate*. You told me about a Crisco party you'd been to the night before in Jersey. A private party. For married men. Men who played golf, owned houses, and barbecued.

You fell in love with me. Or so you said. You wanted to give me an enema. You were like a little kid and made such a scene when I said no. You kept begging. I still said no. You admired my hands. I wouldn't fist you either. No, our love making was nothing out of the ordinary. You were okay. Not great, but okay.

You thought I was talented. You wanted to introduce me to Peter Allen or Tommy Tune. If only I'd come visit you in New York....

We exchanged a few postcards, then you sent me your book inscribed 'For all the good times.'

It gave me a rush seeing your picture like that. Someone I know, I said to myself, someone I've slept with, kissed. My finger traced a frame around your face. Once.

Pierre Trudeau

Sybil Goldstein, Toronto

It was a hot June day in Montreal, 1969, and I was attending grade 9 at Wagar High School in Côte St. Luc, part of Pierre Elliott Trudeau's home riding. He was to attend a constituency meeting there in the evening and address the students in the afternoon. I along with several others had been given the week off in order to decorate the school. I had decided my contribution would be a pastel portrait of him, and I looked through all the back issues of *Time* in the library. At that time, the year of his election, the height of Trudeaumania, I could find only two images of the most important and charismatic man in the country. That was before the Canadian content rulings.

I chose one of him being kissed on the cheek, and spent the better part of a week doing the drawing. Trudeau was introduced by our beloved principal Herr de Groot, who in his enthusiasm forgot his name. I don't remember much of what Trudeau said, it could have been anything. Afterwards he stepped off the podium and started to mix with the students.

There was a mad rush for him. The teachers and security guards immediately joined hands and formed a ring around him. I felt the adrenalin, I had to meet him, I could think of nothing relevant to ask or say. Suddenly, I remembered my drawing. Someone had told me he had stopped and smiled when he saw it posted outside the faculty lounge.

I raced out of the gym, snatched it off the wall and ran back to one of my teachers saying I wanted to give this to Trudeau. He let me through. I walked up to him, mumbled something, presented the picture and smiled. Then it happened. My cheek muscles locked and there was nothing to be done for it. I had to ride out the next precious few moments with a stupid grin on my face. He thanked me and bent down to kiss me. For a brief second I wondered if all the media had been wrong, and this whole kissing thing was really his idea. But then again, at fifteen, I was hardly comfortable initiating intimate contact with grown men. I did however kiss him back on the cheek. I floated outside the ring still smiling and kept that grin on my face until I went to sleep.

A week later I was called to the office. There was an official thank you. It was on gold-embossed P.M. note paper, signed in his flowing fountain hand P.E.T. It was addressed to Sylvia. My name, however, is Sybil.

Pierre Trudeau

David W. Bartlett, Manotick, Ontario

Early in 1950, as a very green graduate, I worked for the old federal Civil Service Commission. In those days, all federal government hiring was handled by the commission. Except for the traditional professions, academic training was suspect: one started from school as a clerk, or from the services as a sergeant, and worked up. However, some of the mandarins had concluded that there might be something to be said for more pre-service training, and had opened a narrow window for university graduates. I was to find these characters – my contemporaries – and persuade the good ones to compete for interesting, though badly paid, government jobs.

One evening, just before her quitting time, the receptionist called to say that an unannounced man had come off the elevator and 'he looks like one of yours.' I asked her to send him up.

What arrived was a bearded young French Canadian who was sounding out the Ottawa job market. We sparred a bit over language, but his English was better than my French so we talked most in English. He told me that he was just back from a visit to China, having spent some time at the London School of Economics and the Sorbonne. Neither beards nor China were as familiar then as they are now. I was planning to spend the next couple of years at the London School, so we talked for an hour or so about his experiences and my prospects. He was obviously very bright, which probably explains why I remember the interview, out of the hundreds which took place in those years.

We agreed that the jobs on my list – customs appraiser and the like – were not really in his line. The External Affairs exam deadline had closed, and he would have to wait for a year. I had however heard by the grapevine that the Treasury and the Prime Minister's Office had a couple of unadvertised appointments that might be interesting, and I made an appointment for him with the Deputy Minister of Finance for the next morning. Finance worked late, I was brash, and things were much more relaxed in those days. When it came to the appointment in the Prime Minister's Office, where I had no contacts but was prepared to try a phone call, he demurred. He allowed that he was off to dinner with a family friend, Mr. St. Laurent (who was then Secretary of State for External Affairs, and was soon to become Prime Minister), and 'perhaps he might raise it with him.' I agreed that this might be a good idea, and after a few more pleasantries he went on his way. I heard no more of him for years.

What struck me at the time was that, until almost the end of our conversation, he had never suggested that he had any political contacts at all. In those days, to drop the name of any obscure MP, especially from Quebec, was an opportunity never to be missed! Not to raise the name of Mr. St. Laurent seemed really extraordinary then, and still seems today.

Anyway, Pierre Trudeau got the job as Assistant Secretary to the Prime Minister, where he served for a couple of years. This is where he must have acquired whatever experience he had of the federal government when he came back much later as the member for Mount Royal, soon to become Prime Minister himself.

Jayne Mansfield

Jean-Paul Yirka, Powell River, British Columbia

'Spiffs.' That's what we called them. Shoes or boots that for one reason or another weren't selling, usually the reason being style or colour. We were offered a bonus to sell them, usually a dollar or two. She bought two pair of shoes and one pair of boots, all spiffs. The boots were made of elephant's ear and were outrageous, especially in her small size, and the shoes were both Italian and equally off the wall.

This was just before noon. I was 'in the back' when I heard my fellow workers jostling and peering out into the front. 'The back' was the storage area of the shoe department (of the Bay) in Vancouver. The guys were gawking at a voluptuous blonde who had just plunked herself down in front of a small crowd standing at a distance. I was intimidated being the one to go out and serve the lady even before I knew that it was Jayne Mansfield. I sat before her on the small fitting stool and as soon as I did I knew I would never be able to get up again! I looked up at the starlet and she realized I was very shy and stunned by the whole scene, her body, etc. Two fellows stood behind her smiling and I almost laughed because they were both wearing black shirts, one with a white tie and one with a silver tie. Great flashy sport coats. Great flashy grins. Bodyguards? Mmm. Actually they were there to buy and pay for her purchases and cart them off.

I was sure she was flirting with me, in my naive innocence. But it was all quite wonderful to me.

Margaret Atwood
Barbara Florio Graham, Gatineau, Quebec

A dozen years ago, when I was a beginning freelancer, working for a local monthly magazine, I received an invitation to a reception preceding an international conference of women writers at Ottawa's National Library.

Arriving at the appointed hour, I discovered that the caterer was just setting up the bar and hors d'oeuvres, and none of the organizers had yet arrived. As I stood alone in the lobby Margaret Atwood came through the doors. At the same time, one of the host group from the library came down the corridor, and went immediately to greet the author.

I joined them, hovering a bit in the background, in awe of my favourite Canadian author, who, I was sure, had no interest in meeting me. But I had underestimated Atwood's grace and courtesy. She asked for directions to the location of her Karsh portrait, which she had not yet seen, and when the library PR person began to describe how to get to the room, I offered to escort Atwood.

By this time, other media and conference attendees had arrived, and Atwood could easily have left me behind as she found someone else to join her. But she ignored everyone else, and chatted pleasantly as we walked, asking me about the magazine I wrote for, and what other kinds of writing I did.

When we reached the room where the Karsh portraits hung, she told me about the sitting. Karsh had posed her in several different positions around her home, and then, unsatisfied with the available backdrops, he picked up a throw rug from the floor and placed it on the wall.

'So many people have asked me about that wall-hanging,' she said, smiling. 'In fact, it looks so terrific like that I probably should take it off the floor and hang it up.'

In subsequent years I've met many more Canadian celebrities, but Margaret Atwood remains the most gracious, unassuming, and kind. I used a quotation of hers in my first book, *Five Fast Steps to Better Writing*, and received a charming letter in response to the copy I sent her.

I'm sure she doesn't recall that writers' conference, but it remains one of my favourite memories.

John Lennon

Mary M. Truitt, Arlington, Virginia

I became a Beatles fan when I was six years old and living in Japan. All my Beatles records were clear red plastic and came from Korea or Indonesia because my father claimed they were cheaper there than in Tokyo. So when he came home from his trips he usually brought a record home with him. The titles of the songs were badly translated: 'Please Mr. Postman' was 'Pleasing Misery Man' and so on. I wandered all over the house with my portable blue record player, stopping every now and then to plug it in and hear a song.

When we finally went to a Beatles concert I sat like a statue in my seat while hundreds of Japanese girls wailed into towels and handkerchiefs and held up pictures of their favourite Beatle. I didn't dare move because I had poison ivy on my arm and I didn't want Paul to see it. I hate to admit it, but yes, my heart belonged to Paul. I took it back a few years later because anyone with any sense at all became adamantly anti-Paul when he grew up and turned out to be so shallow. I can see now that John was the only Beatle to meet. And I did meet him eight years later when I was fourteen and living in Washington, D.C.

A friend's father was helping John with his visa problems and so John was invited to a small cocktail party at their house. My sister and I were invited too, even though most of the party was just adults.

We got there early and stood on the front porch with our friend Marian. We never expected John to arrive on time but as we stood there a black limousine pulled up to the sidewalk.

'I'm going inside,' I said frantically.

'Don't be ridiculous,' said Marian. 'They're really nice.'

John first, with Yoko right behind him, came snaking up the twisting cement stairs. 'Marian,' called John with his hand held up in a wave.

'Hi John, hi Yoko,' said Marian coolly. As they got closer she said, 'I'd like you to meet two friends of mine, Alexandra and Mary Truitt.'

As I shook hands with John, and then Yoko, all I kept thinking was if nothing else ever happens to me my whole life at least I met John Lennon. Marian offered to take them inside and just before

119

they went through the door John turned back and said, 'You're not leaving, are you?'

'No,' Alex and I jumped to say.

'Great,' said John with a warm smile. 'We'll see you inside.'

As soon as the screen door slammed we pressed ourselves against the window and looked in to see him meeting everyone else.

John was wearing a beautiful velvet suit, a deep sea blue. With it he wore a white shirt and skinny black tie. He wasn't particularly tall and I was surprised to find his hair was reddish blonde. It was medium long, straight and parted in the middle. He had on those little Granny glasses you always see him wearing in pictures and some of the time he wore a black beret. He kept joking around with everyone he met and laughing at his own jokes and bouncing up and down to some beat of his own.

Yoko was not a bit like John. She was conservative – she didn't put out and she didn't want anything from you. Her thick, and I do mean thick, black hair was parted in the middle revealing little of her face and fell around her body like a protective cape; with her black clothes you couldn't tell where her hair ended and she began. If it weren't for her smile, which transformed her occasionally, she would have seemed a strange, blank creature.

I was light-headed from the drinks and dizzy with my independence. John and Yoko began to pass around presents to everyone and I went over to see if I could have one too. They were giving away a single.

'Why are you giving these away?' I asked.

'Because it's important for little girls like you to listen to what we're saying and pay attention. You have to listen to the words. This record is called "Woman Is the Nigger of the World."'

'What's that supposed to mean?' I asked.

'Listen to the record and find out,' he said. 'We're giving this away because no one will buy it and it's important for people to know what's really happening in the world.' John signed my record and drew a face. 'You must ask Yoko to sign it too,' he said.

'That's okay,' I said. 'I just wanted you to sign it.'

He pointed over to where Yoko was standing and said more firmly, 'You have to ask her to sign it too. We're both on the record and you don't want to hurt her feelings.'

Although I didn't care whether Yoko signed my record or not, I went because obviously John wanted me to go. Yoko was happy to autograph my record and also drew a face.

'If John drew a face, I'll draw one for you too,' she said.

I showed John. This was when the drinks I'd had began to show. 'John,' I said. 'I've loved the Beatles all my life since I was six.' 'You're too young to be a Beatles fan,' he said. 'No, I'm not,' I said. I was rather insulted he didn't believe me. 'I've lived in Japan and had all your records and then I saw you in a concert there.' 'You were at a concert,' he said. 'Try one of my cigarettes. These are French. You'll like them better than those.' He pointed to my pack of Winston's. Obviously he was bored when he was the subject of the conversation. The cigarettes he chain-smoked all night were Gauloises Blues and they smelled like cigars. I took one from his crumpled pack, put it in my blue jean pocket and then put one of my own up to his waiting lighter.

'That's strange,' he said. 'I give you a cigarette and you put it in your pocket and smoke one of your own.'

I was rather embarrassed because I had hoped he wouldn't see me do that trick. The drinks had made me think I was invisible. 'I wanted a souvenir,' I said.

'Then here,' he said, holding out the pack to me. 'Take another and smoke that one.' I took another. 'And here.' He reached into his pocket. 'Take whatever you want.' His palm held a treasure chest of things to choose from besides American and English coins. John kept laughing. He was enjoying himself and seemed to think everything was such a great big joke. I took a tortoise-shell guitar pick and a red glass button that shined like a ruby. 'You're sure that's all you want?' he said. I nodded. 'Good,' he said. 'We got that out of the way so now we can talk.'

'I've loved you all my life,' I continued to talk like an idiot.

'Don't be silly,' he said. He didn't seem to understand. He didn't want me to love him. At that moment I felt lost all the way and happened to look across the room and see Yoko. She had that transforming smile on her face and to my surprise she winked at me very deliberately. I was rather taken aback, but I smiled at her crookedly and thought she couldn't possibly have known what I was talking about with John. But I was saved.

John kept laughing at me in a nice way, he hadn't seen Yoko wink, and kept repeating that I was too young to be a Beatles fan when my sister and another friend came up and asked John to sign their arms. We all pulled up our sleeves and John went to work with a ballpoint pen until we were all tattooed in his wormy script.

Then a man came up – a manager or something – and tapped John on the shoulder and said it was time for him to go. Yoko was already waiting by the door. 'Can I kiss John good-bye?' I asked the man, because he seemed to be in charge. 'No,' he said. 'Yoko gets jealous.' She didn't look jealous to me, she was just smiling that saintly smile and waiting calmly.

'I meant on the cheek,' I said, but no one was listening. John's attention was turned towards the door and I noticed a certain panic seemed to overtake him – as if he wasn't going to make it there, as if someone might try and stop him from leaving. My last sight of John was his back, as smooth and blue as a whale's, as he was escorted out of the room surrounded by a sea of people.

Jacqueline Kennedy Onassis

Richard Grayson, Davie, Florida

One day in September 1972, a week before I was to enter my senior year at Brooklyn College, I drove up to Manhattan to visit my grandmother in New York Hospital. The week before, Grandma had been bleeding internally and had actually died for a minute or so before the doctors revived her. She seemed to be doing pretty well now. 'Grandma, I didn't expect to see you looking so well,' I told her, and she replied, 'Honey, you didn't expect to see me at all.'

It was one of those dry, mild, gorgeous end-of-summer afternoons and when I left the hospital I decided – since I had a legal parking space – to take a walk. I walked west until I got to Fifth Avenue, and then I entered the park.

I was lost in thought. I'd never had anyone close to me die, and my grandmother's brush with death frightened and disturbed me. How would I take it when someone I loved really died? And I was thinking about college and how I would soon have to leave the security of being an undergraduate. Should I apply to law schools? Should I get an MA in English? Would I have to get a job? Could I?

Suddenly I heard a woman cry, 'Look out!' and I turned around quickly. I'd been walking in such an aimless, thoughtless path that this woman on a bicycle had only just managed to avoid colliding with me. In a second, as if coming out of a dream, I realized that she was Jacqueline Kennedy Onassis. Riding on another bike slightly behind her was her son, John F. Kennedy, Jr., a boy of twelve or thirteen.

They stopped for a moment, and Mrs. Onassis asked me, 'Are you all right?'

'I'm sorry,' I babbled, 'I wasn't looking.'

She nodded. Then she looked at her son with a knowing glance, and they started away on their bikes again.

'I'm sorry!' I shouted as they cycled away. They didn't look back. 'I've got to be more careful,' I said aloud – to myself.

I had once seen Mrs. Onassis a couple of years before on the street. At that time I was walking towards her and nodded in recognition but didn't make any attempt to speak to her or call attention to her. She seemed grateful and nodded back at me then. But this time, Mrs. Onassis had actually spoken to me. She had spoken first. 'Look out!' she had said. And: 'Are you all right?'

Walking out of the park, driving back to Brooklyn, lying in my bed that night, I decided that no one had ever given me such good advice or had shown more concern for my well-being.

Tennessee Williams
Katharine Fehl, New York City

Tennessee said to me: 'Writing is very difficult, isn't it, Mees Feehl!' It was quite a moment. Very serious. Frontal, with a great weight which would have rendered the moment memorable even if he had not been who he was.

At the suggestion of my agent and friend, Michael Kingman, I had gone over to see him at the Elysee Hotel, where he kept a suite. I was looking for a play to do at the 79th Street Boat Basin and thought he might have one for me. What the hey, right?

The plan had been to pick him up and then go out for lunch. But he said he had fallen down and suggested having lunch there with him instead. He was shorter, stronger, stockier and much handsomer than I'd expected. He had his beard on, and a rather nice robe.

We ordered BLTs and Cokes and sat on his bed and watched *Hamlet* on TV. We laughed a lot. I didn't think it was such a hot production. It had Claire Bloom as Gertrude and I don't remember who else, and it was prosaic and okay. But he was so grateful for and aware of the enormous phenomenon of the play that he was less concerned with evaluating the production than I, or he was more resigned to the probability of relative mediocrity and this was rather decent. He was punctiliously polite, almost officious, and he carried his importance like a visible thing that he knew I could see and that he had to move around him to sit down, like the train of a king's robe.

So we talked about new plays he was working on and how the critics had been out to slaughter him lately – the last few years – and how I would go down to Key West and stay with him and he would sort through some scripts. He also suggested that *Camino Real* might – would – work beautifully out there in the open at the Boat Basin. Camino with the accent on the Cam.

But, he said, you must check with my agent (at that time Mitch Douglas) at ICM. We spoke of Audrey Wood, speaking of agents. I had just directed a reading of a Carson McCullers mishmash, which Audrey Wood had come over to New Dramatists to see. Incredibly tiny and rude, with a rudeness that immediately declared itself to be of legendary stature, and thus charming. She seemed to have the conceit that it was a logical rudeness, the product of economy. He said he had not spoken to her in eleven years and was clearly eager for any detail about her, any gesture I could reproduce, even my critical comments about her, which he then distilled and correlated with his own image of her.

Anyway, he knew absolutely nothing about me, knew not that I had the slightest interest in anything beyond producing plays. That I had enormous pretensions as a writer of plays was not the part of me for which he had been prepared. So when he came out with the line about writing, 'Writing is very difficult, isn't it, Mees Feehl?', I was the more moved and nearly responsive from that place of true self that is always visible but rarely a functional part of the persona. The part that was watching, knowing damn well its own contempt for cowtowing to other writers, adulating their success, or worse for God's sake – making oneself small in order to use their importance to make oneself feel important.

As he said this line about writing being difficult, just as I was leaving, and gave me an impaling look ... I looked at him and stuttered, feeling my presumption. 'Yes,' I said, 'yes.' Many things occurred during the fleeting moment. One of those which actually comprises but a few seconds and yet provides fuel for many trains of thought, for many epiphanies.

I thought, 'I'm forced to acknowledge that I'm a "writer" – oh, heavenly father, where do I turn?' I suppose this thought alone carries no threat, but it instantly extends itself to say, 'Now I must indeed write.' And all of this seemed to me to be incorporated in this writer's lucid simple question; and it was with a sense of collusion and with a challenge that he looked at me, I swear it. I'm getting feverish now, as I insist that he held that much in his voice and eyes as he looked at me, and I stuttered back.

M.M. & Arthur Miller

Nicholas Delbanco, Ann Arbor, Michigan

In the late fifties, when I was in high school, my father took me to the theatre. John Gielgud brought a one-man show to Manhattan that he called *The Ages of Man*. We had good seats. This was a rare occasion, and my father knew it. My elder brother was away, my younger brother too young; my mother had stayed home. So it was just the two of us, enjoined to a kind of companionable silence – watching the theatregoers, then the curtain, the way other fathers and sons might study a thicket or stream. I followed the usher down the aisle with a sense of growing importance; we were fifth or sixth row centre, three and four seats in. I wore my suit, my best shirt. I had shined my shoes, I took the seat nearer the aisle. The two to my right remained vacant; the lights dimmed.

Gielgud began with the sonnets and stood above us declaiming. Three or four minutes into his performance, a couple arrived at my right. They were not ushered in. The woman was wearing a pink suit, was blonde and wore dark glasses; I remember thinking that the dark glasses were strange. The theatre had grown dark already, after all; perhaps her eyes were bad. She folded herself next to me; then her tall consort sat. 'Rough winds do shake the darling buds of May,' said Gielgud, 'And summer's lease hath all too short a date.' The man's face seemed familiar. He wore horn-rimmed glasses, had a strong nose and deeply lined cheeks; he was, I realized, the playwright Arthur Miller. We had just been reading *Death of a Salesman* in school. The woman wore perfume. With what I can only describe as the force of revelation, I jolted to the certainty that the lady to my right, his left, was Marilyn Monroe. Our knees were near. She would have come into the darkened house to keep autograph hounds at bay; she sought me out, sat down. Our hands could touch. Gielgud continued intoning; the others seemed impervious; the world was rearranged. Two minutes before intermission they left, donning dark glasses once more; I hugged my secret to me for the twenty-minute wait. Then – with the curtain up again, and once again in darkness – they returned. I said, 'Excuse me,' and lifted my program; I had placed it carefully across the waiting seat. She smiled. She said, 'Hello.' I had my father with me, great artistry in front of us, a playwright to my right; we were listening to Shakespeare and we heard the words together.

Years later, lightning struck my kitchen in Vermont. It came in through the open door, spot-welded the simmering pot to the stove, short-circuited the dishwasher, exploded the lights and, crackling, spurting, left. This was like that.

Glenn Gould

Linda Rogers, Toronto

Crouched in the seventh row of the Stratford Festival Theatre, dressed in something far too cocktail for a sixteen-year-old, holding my little clutch purse bulging with Clearasil, Maybelline mascara and my mother's written orders and procedures should I be approached by a man with hard candy, I held my breath and waited.

Eventually he arrived, scarf, gloves, woollen hat, long underwear, several pairs of socks, and yelled into the dark and empty space where the audience he hated would eventually sit, that the air conditioning had to be turned off. This God-like adjustment of the weather affected me in a way I later learned to recognize as orgasmic. I was carrying a pretty heavy current and he hadn't even touched the piano.

It's July, twenty-six years later. Now he is dead, of course, and I am listening to his CBC recording of some Mozart piano concertos, just to get in the mood. I wish I could remember what he played that afternoon. Be assured, it was gorgeous.

I was practically in a coma, didn't even notice when he removed his fingers from the keys, pushed back the bench, jumped off the stage, took seven giant steps and discreetly coughed. I looked up. Oh my God. The day before I ate French fries. I was breaking out. I mean, right there, at that very moment. There are times when your whole life passes in front of your half-inch glasses. So many French fries, so little piano practice. I hated my mother at that moment. Why didn't she make me? Why did she let me slouch around with Katy Keene comics, dreaming of bouffant dresses when I could have been learning sonatas?

It was very obvious we were going to have a conversation. What was I going to say to Glenn Gould?

'What are you doing here?' he asked. A reasonable question.

I couldn't tell him I dropped my program at a performance of *Coriolanus* the night before and found myself locked in a jack-knife position. Besides, I didn't know about backache in 1961.

'I love you,' I said, stupidly, as I have said, equally stupidly, several times since, to others. Well, I guess it was true. At that moment, I loved him, his power to make something beautiful for God and a sixteen-year-old girl.

He told me I had to leave, then left with me. We got in his red convertible and drove, fast. In retrospect I long for 'The Journal' or the six o'clock news. There was no one there to record my fabulous ride through Stratford, Ontario, with the greatest pianist of the day and nobody believes it. I have a reputation for fiction and I don't think he had a reputation for picking up little girls.

He bought me an ice cream, then took me to a small hotel. We watched a cowboy show on a small black-and-white TV in the lobby. Never went upstairs. Then he took me home, or rather to the boarding house where I was living by the grace and favour of the Canada Council. I wish I'd touched him. He didn't even take off his gloves. Not once. My children are musical. I wonder how that happened.

Stan Brakhage
Joy Walker, Toronto

In 1965 I decided if I were ever to become the painter I wanted to be I had to go to New York City. So I left home and took the train from Troutdale, Oregon, and points smaller, across the U.S. About the time we crossed the Great Divide, a large man with a dark head of hair got on the train and asked if he could sit with me. There were many other seats in the car but I was flattered and needed someone to talk to, so began a long conversation that lasted until we reached New York. Neither of us had sleepers (I still like to travel that way: looking, talking, reading, eating and sleeping in the same spot!) so he talked and I listened, mostly about New York and all the artists he knew there. He talked about his neighbour Robert Creeley and how he didn't like to fly either, members of Fluxus were mentioned. He gave me addresses of two or three people, Charlotte Moorman and Carolee Schneeman were two I remember. I was too shy and intimidated to ever call on these artists, but nevertheless I felt I had been introduced to my new life! I had only the vaguest notion of who Stan Brakhage was or what he did and was even less informed about the artists he discussed. On his part, he must have been intrigued by the naive country girl who had barely been in a big city before going off to live in the biggest one.

Thirteen years later, after S.B. gave a lecture-movie showing at the Art Gallery of Ontario in Toronto, I went up afterwards to thank him for giving me such a good start and to tell him that, yes, I was a painter now. Although he smiled, it was clear from his puzzled look that I was the only one who needed to remember.

Errol Flynn

Brian C. Greggains, West Hill, Ontario

In 1952 a real estate developer from Jamaica went to London to see if he could interest some well-heeled Brits in buying some of the land he was holding. He approached the public relations department of the London Press Exchange, then the largest ad agency in the U.K. I was on the staff as a senior account executive.

After my boss agreed to take on the assignment I was handed the job of implementing it.

Straight publicity seemed the obvious answer, but how to bait the hook? The sophisticated London journalists we hoped to attract were not sitting around waiting for a chance to flog beach lots in Jamaica.

Research disclosed the names of some of the better-known people who owned homes or property on the island. One of them was Errol Flynn. By coincidence, Flynn happened to be in London making a movie.

Flynn agreed to come to a press party. We got together a list of press people to invite and prepared a nice invitation announcing that there were still some marvellous properties to be had in Jamaica and Errol Flynn would be there at the party to say so.

We had a good turnout. To set the tone we served only champagne cocktails. When most of our invitees had arrived, in came Flynn and a small entourage. He was wearing a sports jacket, a dark Viyella shirt and a woollen tie. And he was glowering. I led him to a chair more or less away from the press who had to be restrained from mobbing him. We poured a champagne cocktail into him and then another.

Only when he had finished his second drink did I approach him again. In my most polite London public relations voice I said, 'Mr. Flynn, do you think I could bring over some of the press in a minute?' He knew why he was there and that our invitations had said he would be prepared to talk about glorious Jamaica.

He turned his face slowly towards me, glared at me, and slumped back in his chair. 'Don't bother me, Buster,' he snarled. 'I've had a hard day.'

Fielding Dawson

David McFadden, Toronto

Here's irony you can cut with a knife but you have to let it unravel a bit first. I'm not going to make a big thing out of it but there's tragedy here too. The sensitive reader will detect it and I'm not going to pander to the other kind.

Fielding Dawson is my favourite American writer bar none. But the only time I met him was before he had become so, although it was after he had already written most of the books that I later learned to love, the *Krazy Kat* stories, the *Penny Lane* novels, *The Sun Rises into the Sky, The Man Who Changed Overnight, A Great Day for a Ballgame, The Greatest Story Ever Told* ... all of that.

One time I was reading *The Greatest Story Ever Told* on a bus running from Kamloops to Wawa and a tiresome lady sitting next to me was going on and on about how nice it was to be sitting next to a good clean Christian gentleman.

But that was a few years after my premature meeting with the man who had not yet become my hero, Fielding Dawson, which took place at a book-launch at the Spadina Hotel. He used to come up to Toronto in those days. Never does now. All of a sudden he comes up to me and introduces himself, a little blonde guy with long hair and flushed with boozy enthusiasm, and he says he knows who I am and wants me to know he read my book and thought it was terrific but it sort of tailed off towards the end.

It was a strange moment for me. I immediately liked the guy although I hadn't read his books yet and only vaguely knew his name but he exhibited what I at the time considered the unbearable arrogance of Yankees in foreign countries. Put it down to immaturity but I was a true Canadian and didn't want to hear from some uppity Yankee Doodle Dandy up here on a visit that my book tailed off at the end. In fact the book didn't tail off at the end, it tailed off at the beginning.

I should have been delighted he'd read the book and I should have bought him a drink and spent the next few days showing him around Toronto, taking him to the zoo and everything, but I was an over-sensitive poet with a sneer a foot long about anything American. Not like that at all now of course.

So I just gave Fielding a big brush-off, a cold stare, and walked away. Brush-offs of unrecognized genius. A while later I became entranced with his books. Turned a lot of Canadians on to his work. One person in particular to whom I recommended his work at a critical point in her life still considers me a genius for having done so. I never met Fielding Dawson since that first time and have never heard a peep from him even though I have sent him clippings of articles in which I'd mentioned his work from time to time along with little notes of appreciation. Then I heard that one of the editors of this *Brushes with Greatness* book sent Fielding a note requesting a contribution from him and he replied in a thoroughly unpleasant way, saying he wouldn't even consider contributing to such a dumb project.

Martha Graham

Rebecca Vories, Denver, Colorado

When I was twenty I left my small town in western Colorado and took a job as a cashier in a drugstore in Aspen. In order not to feel like such a hick I invented an accent which I called Dutch. I hoped no one from Holland would show up. I wanted to pretend to be interesting and from elsewhere, just like everyone else.

One evening I waited on a very elegant and dramatic-looking woman and her companion. As they were paying for their sundries, the woman remarked on my accent and told me that I had an unusual and beautiful face. I was pleased, of course.

The next day I flushed with embarrassment upon reading the announcement in the local paper that Martha Graham and her troupe had arrived in town and there I saw a picture of the lady who had complimented me so nicely.

Prior to then, I had never seen a dance performance. But I later moved to New York to work and went to see Martha Graham and her troupe at every possible opportunity, always feeling a special connection. That brief encounter at the age of twenty started a lifelong interest in dance, if only as a spectator. Even to this day, whenever I feel unattractive, I remember that Martha Graham didn't think so.

The Archbishop of Canterbury

Anthony LaViola, Toronto

A world-wide Anglican conference was being held at the University of Western Ontario in the summer of 1965 and the students in residence at Huron College were sharing space with bishops from all over the world.

One evening, after a particularly intensive study session, a friend and I decided to go for a walk in order to clear our heads. It was one of those hot muggy July evenings so we decided to walk through the cooler lower corridors. We rounded a corner and by chance ran into the Archbishop of Canterbury, Michael Ramsay, and his wife. They were standing in front of a Coke machine with mystified looks on their faces.

As we approached the Archbishop noticed us and said, 'How do you use this machine?'

'You just put a dime in the slot,' I replied, 'and a Coke comes out the bottom.'

He pulled out a handful of Canadian coins and said, 'What's a dime?' I took one from his hand, showed it to him, then inserted it in the machine and got him his Coke.

A short but interesting discussion ensued, in which we talked about the various slang names for British and Canadian money. The Archbishop's wife added some gracious and amusing remarks and we parted.

After this encounter, when I would see him in the corridors he would smile and say hello. It was encouraging to see that even the great have not-so-great frustrations with modern life.

Greta Garbo

Ross Skoggard, New York City

One day during the sixties I noticed a woman walking up the hill on Lexington Avenue. She had on a square-shouldered sealskin coat from the forties like one my mother used to wear. That's why I watched her. She was wearing white Keds and glasses. She walked very butch, swinging her shoulders and glancing intently from the ground, to the shops at her left and back. She looked like she was about to start talking to herself out loud any minute. With the sneakers, the walk, and the intense expression I had her made as one of those upper middle-class lunatics you see a lot on the upper east side.

I was listening to what my college roommate walking next to me was saying, but I didn't take my eyes off this woman. Maybe I missed my mom. Her grey hair was cut in a page boy. She wore no makeup. Her face was very lined, but as she passed I saw her perfect profile, unmistakable.

'That was Greta Garbo,' I told my roommate.

'You're full of it.'

We walked on. 'That was Greta Garbo. Want to bet?'

We turned around and I started walking fast. She was walking fast. I had to run. I caught up. I walked beside her, looking at her. She saw me but didn't acknowledge me.

'Excuse me, but aren't you Greta ...?' She didn't stop, she didn't look at me, didn't make it easy.

'... Garbo?' She winced a bit, nodded her head rapidly.

'I just wanted to say I'm a great fan.' Only then did Garbo look at me. She seemed relieved, maybe grateful, that I wasn't going to rip a piece off her.

My roommate caught up to me. 'It's her,' I said.

Garbo crossed 68th Street and stood on the corner waiting to cross Lex. Nobody else knew who she was. Her identity was a secret we shared. A secret she could trust me with. Knowing who she was and not making her pay for it, I felt I was performing an act of friendship. I felt she liked me.

Bob Hope
Michael Herr, London, England

December, 1967.

They'd fixed up a corner of the Command helicopter with pillows to make the short ride more comfortable for him. He strapped in, had a word with his producer, and then, as the rotors started, he stuffed cotton into his ears and leaned back. Before the ship had reached a thousand feet he was out. He wasn't sleeping deeply. He was resting on some shelf of privacy that he must have learned to reach quickly and directly through long practice, travelling and performing as hard as he did, and had done, for thirty years.

Famous beyond famous, the ultimate show-business machine, when you met him you could look and stare and still not really see him. Your real life was just another medium that he was starring in. But while he slept and I watched, something began happening to his face. The laughing aggression dissolved first into gentleness and then into a melting tenderness. Even the skin tone changed, and his face filled with what I could only call longing, although what he could still be longing for after his attainments, I don't know.

If you saw him in a sketch wearing a dress and wig and heels, you'd never think for a moment that you were looking at a woman, but he looked very feminine now. (Raquel Welch was sitting two seats away, providing a strong point of reference.) He cocked his head as though he was straining to hear something that was just a little too far away, and his hands began to move slowly, drifting back and forth like a soft-shoe dancer's hands. His smile grew even sweeter. I couldn't recall the leer that I thought had always been his only smile.

He was a wonderful dancer anyway, always underrated there. He expressed things in his dancing that were repressed and even strangled in his comedy, and even though he was only moving his hands now, the motion was so beautiful and soothing that I couldn't stop looking. I felt that I should but I couldn't, while years and layers of cover came away from him and there was nothing left in the icon face that I recognized. Except that I knew it was him. The name-in-the-face was still intact.

A few minutes later the helicopter started its descent and one of his people leaned across and touched his shoulder. His hands stopped. Looking at them now, I could believe that he had boxed with them. He opened his eyes and saw me. He was like a man snapping shut a secret album because someone had just come into the room. His features lengthened and sharpened, the old were-wolf effect, and he was already running through the lines he would be speaking in a few minutes, the lines that disgusted me that day and make me laugh now, and seem so touching.

Well, here we are in Bien Hoa. Bien Hoa ... that's Vietnamese for 'Duck!' But say, what a reception I got at the airport. They thought I was a replacement....

I was back dissociating again, much better in wartime. The old soft-shoe man was out, repossessed by Bob Hope, and in those few seconds I lost all interest in him.

Jawaharlal Nehru

George Cadogan, Guelph, Ontario

With packsack and sleeping bag I was in India in the spring of 1939, eight years before independence. The Indian National Congress was the great political party. I went by train to Tripuri where the annual congress session was to be held. After getting down from the train I had miles to walk but I had plenty of company. More than a hundred thousand followers of Gandhi were making their way to the village.

The first morning I got up from my pallet and headed for the nearest water tap. While I stood waiting to wash I recognized the man ahead of me. Jawaharlal Nehru shared the same basic facilities as the most humble untouchable. When he finished his ablutions another congress official arrived and they chatted while I splashed water on my face. I was too awestruck to speak to Nehru and I wouldn't have dared interrupt while he was talking to another official.

The spiritual leader, Mohandas Gandhi, was also in attendance, but he was confined to a temporary hospital hut with a raging fever. A huge billboard was fashioned high above the hospital where a graph showed the rise and fall of Gandhi's temperature, with a new line added every six hours.

The Dalai Lama

Kim Rosenberg, Toronto

The Dalai Lama paid a visit to Canada in the winter of 1981. His first stop was Toronto, at the Old Town Hall at the corner of King and Jarvis, where he met with the Tibetan community. He wore robes and a large cloth hat or crown of fine brocade and sat upon a raised throne.

Next came a public audience which was attended by about five hundred Westerners, many of whom were familiar to me as practising Buddhists. For us Canadians, unused to the pomp of the Tibetan spiritual hierarchy, His Holiness appeared in the plain, dark maroon robes of a simple monk and sat in a low chair at the front of the large room. As this was his first visit to Canada, and the first time many of us had seen him, there was a great deal of excitement and expectation. His Holiness shattered this tension with the first line of his address: 'Well, you see, actually I'm very tired and as there is not much to say in any case, perhaps I'll just wish you good night.'

At that point two things happened. First, there was an almost tangible deflation of the energy shared by the crowd coupled with a deep sense of disappointment. The very next moment I perceived a brilliant flash of light followed by a wave of compassion which emanated from His Holiness, who then continued: 'Well, perhaps I could say something.' But I was too overcome by this deeper communication to pay much attention to his following words.

Later I spoke to many of the people in attendance and they all confirmed they had experienced the disappointment followed by some kind of vision and a sense of compassion. Instead of a flash of light, some had seen His Holiness as the bodhisattva of compassion, Chenresig (of whom the Dalai Lama is said to be an emanation). Some had seen Je Tsong Khapa, the founder of the Dalai Lama's sect. That His Holiness touched us all in a very personal way was apparent, but exactly what he did I cannot say. Buddhists say that disappointment is the one emotion that the ego can do nothing with. Perhaps His Holiness deflated our egos by severing our false expectations of him and thus off guard he could truly expose to us his enlightened mind. Whatever the case may be, that this simple and beautiful man deeply affects those who meet him is without doubt.

Muhammad Ali

Joyce Carol Oates

My single brief encounter with the man whose face had been, in his prime, and not many years ago, one of the great iconographic images of the era – reputedly known and honoured in parts of the world in which likenesses of the Pope and the United States President would have gone unrecognized – took place in a crowded restaurant in a swankily tacky resort-casino hotel in Atlantic City, on the Boardwalk, at approximately 9 a.m., Saturday, January 23, 1988. Seated at a table some fifteen feet from the 'great' man (the quotation marks don't indicate irony in terms of the man, only in terms of 'greatness' itself), my husband and I saw that there came to his table an intermittent but steady stream of admirers, autograph-seekers, and well-wishers as he sat with two friends eating breakfast. Fascinating to observe how celebrity thrives on being recognized: 'celebrated.' How, in this case sui generis the continuous surrender of privacy had become ritualized, a way perhaps of establishing existence. Men approached the great man's table, bent to speak to him, shook his hand, asked for autographs; white and black men both. Two sportily dressed black women approached the table and, after paying homage to him, traded jokes with his two companions. A white man came over and asked him to pose with his two small sons for a photograph, and, hugging the little boys on either side, he managed to smile, rather stiffly – his face was usually expressionless – and looked, for that moment, almost animated. I wondered what sort of immortality we hope for by being linked, if just on a fading Polaroid print, with one whose 'greatness' has so visibly begun to decline into mortality.

I asked my husband if he thought I should go over too to ask for an autograph, and he said yes of course – why not? In this context it seemed not only a courteous but a necessary gesture; even a loving one. (I should say parenthetically that I had never asked anyone for an autograph before, nor had I ever wanted one, for 'greatness' in the public sense means nothing to me. I wish it did.) So I made my way to his table, and made my shy, self-conscious request, and he took up silently the ballpoint pen I offered, and positioned it above the sheet of hotel note paper I offered, impassive, simply waiting for me to tell him my name and the date, and then in a slow deliberate unfaltering hand he signed his name; and I thanked him, and murmured a few inadequate words, and then to my surprise and embarrassment tears sprang from my eyes and ran down my cheeks, as if I'd been clapped hard on the back, the sheer shock of it, the pain, seeing this famous face up close as I did, seeing that the skin wasn't so leaden as it appeared from a distance, the eyes weren't so dull and without expression but really rather warm, shining, living, yes and in a way young too, and I apologized, and walked quickly out of the restaurant, leaving him and his companions staring after me in amazement. 'Crazy white woman,' they might have murmured, and changed the subject.

My husband was waiting for me outside and he too looked rather embarrassed. A public breakdown, however minor and temporary, isn't what I would like to consider my 'style.' But there it was, in our possession, hardly a rarity, but precious.

Edward G. Robinson
Charles Wilkins, Dundas, Ontario

Just before Christmas, 1978, I took a train from Valencia to Madrid. I had been travelling Europe for the better part of a year, and had just come through an intense but disappointing affair with an American woman on the Costa Del Sol. I took a room near the Generalissimo's palace and spent most of two days in bed.

On Christmas Eve, I walked through a light rain to the Prado and found my way to a high-ceilinged gallery that housed a dozen or so El Grecos. My only company was a dignified old man, a kind of Prospero figure, with white hair and a linen-coloured goatee. He wore a three-piece suit, and was examining one of the paintings with a magnifying glass. As I came up behind him, he turned to me and I recognized him as the gangster actor, Edward G. Robinson. I spoke to him, and he responded with a brief, exuberant lecture on the paintings around us. He commented on the variety of their colour and their depth of spirit. But he was most concerned about a particular quality of light that he was unable to define. He used the words 'dispersal' and 'longing' but couldn't quite put them into context. Eventually he looked at me and, in a last attempt to convey what he meant, said, 'Think about the rain ... then think about this room.' He gestured to the ornate ceiling, which could barely be seen above the lights.

When I was about to leave, he said, 'What's your name?' I told him and he gave me his hand and said, 'I'm Edward Robinson.' I told him I knew, and he nodded and went back to his magnifying glass.

A few days later, a student told me that Robinson was a prodigious art collector and scholar, and was well known as a benefactor to young artists. He lived reclusively in an apartment in central Madrid.

In mid-January I went to Paris. On my first morning there, I bought the *International Tribune* and went into a restaurant for breakfast. On the back page was a lengthy obituary for Edward G. Robinson. I read it, feeling faintly etherized, then read the rest of the paper, which seemed to have been written by someone who viewed the world through the reducing end of a peepscope. That night I tore out the obituary and trimmed its edges with a pair of nail scissors that I carried in my pack. I stared at it for a few seconds and stuffed it in the pocket of my jeans.

By the beginning of February I had returned to the Costa Del Sol where I was sharing a villa with a number of Americans. One morning several of us walked to the beach to play touch football. On the play that ended the game I ran a few feet into the water chasing an overthrown pass and ended up diving into the surf in my T-shirt and jeans. Later at the villa I pulled the soggy obituary from my back pocket. Edward G.'s picture was smudged to the point that his homburg appeared to have lifted from his head. I carefully unfolded the wad of newsprint and plastered it to the stucco of the living-room wall. A few days later it would be scraped off in bran flake-sized bits by a cleaning woman whom we'd hired to guarantee our damage deposit. But for the time being it clung there, a reminder of last month's urgency, half dissolved in sea water.

In the months that followed, I read more about Edward G. Robinson's reclusiveness. He apparently spent the last months of his life in all but total seclusion. I grew to believe that I was the last person to have conversed with him – at least about anything that he cared about. I hold that belief to this day.

Have You Had a Brush With Greatness?

The response to our request for anecdotes for *Brushes With Greatness* was so enthusiastic that we are now in the planning stages of *Brushes With Greatness, Volume II*. If you've had an experience that you would like to tell us about, simply forward your anecdote (we prefer that it be no more than two pages in length), along with your complete name, address and telephone number, to:

Brushes With Greatness, Volume II
Coach House Press
401 Huron Street (rear)
Toronto, Ontario
M5S 2G5

We encourage you to mention any 'artifacts' you may have obtained as a result of your 'brush' (e.g., a photo, gift, or autograph). A reproduction of the item would be great, but do not send the original!

We regret that we cannot guarantee a response to your submission, nor the return of any material. All authors' royalties from the sale of *Volume II* will be donated to Amnesty International.

Editors for the Press: Russell Banks,
Michael Ondaatje and David Young

For a list of other books,
write for our catalogue
or call (416) 979-7374.

The Coach House Press
401 (rear) Huron Street
Toronto, Canada M5S 2G5